HEIRS
OF
DARKNESS

HEIRS
OF
DARKNESS

Zilpha Keatley Snyder

ATHENEUM

New York

1978

Library of Congress Cataloging in Publication Data

Snyder, Zilpha Keatley.
    Heirs of darkness.
    I. Title.
PZ4.S6758He   [PS3569.N97]   813'.5'4   78-53799
ISBN 0-689-10913-X

To Larry, Libby, Olive and Italy

HEIRS
OF
DARKNESS

1

"Y o u r little boy?" The pink-suited woman was leaning across the aisle, smiling benevolently. Her curiosity had been obvious since she had boarded the bus in San Francisco and now at last it was beyond control.

Paul was kneeling on the seat staring through the window, his eyes intently focused, lips moving in silent dialogue. Totally absorbed as he so often was in some private, inner experience, he was completely unaware of Beth's scrutiny as well as the avid stare from across the aisle. Following his gaze, Beth saw an occasional clump of gray-green trees or an outcropping of rock, relieving a monotony of grassy, sunbleached hills. Nothing, it would seem, that could hold a four-year-old's rapt attention. The woman's question still hung in the air, and Beth turned to answer it.

"Yes, he's mine," she said, smile spread thin over resentment. The woman was resentable, round eyes gleaming with greedy curiosity, color-coordinated face, only a shade paler than her pantsuit, quivering with the need to confirm her suspicions. It was clear that she thought there was something wrong with Paul.

"Lovely child." The smile sweetened further. "Beautiful eyes." A pause and then, "How old is he?"

"He'll be five in October."

"Oh really?" The pink benevolence flared briefly towards surprise before dropping back to simper. "He seems—younger," and then, as if suddenly aware of tactlessness, hurrying to make amends, she beamed, "and you seem quite young, my dear, to have a five-year-old child."

It was a compliment that Beth had heard before, and always with mixed feelings, among them the suspicion that the speaker was reacting to something other than physical appearance—to some interior thing, ungrown and tentative, where there should have been the sure and stable center of maturity. But now she found, to her surprise, that her answering smile was at least halfway sincere. It would be good to feel young—carefree—again, after these last few weeks.

"I'm older than I look," she said inanely—managing at least not to say, "I'm thirty," to abjectly offer up privileged information in gratitude for a demeaning compliment from a plump, pink woman in polyester knit.

"Lucky you. Wish I could say the same. Will he be in kindergarten, then, in the fall—your little boy?"

"Yes, in the fall, unless—" Reminding herself about blabbering, Beth stopped, but the woman's eyes widened eagerly, and Beth realized that the "unless" had confirmed her suspicions. Now she was certain there was something wrong with Paul.

"—unless there's no kindergarten near enough to where we'll be living," she finished quickly. "We'll be living on a ranch, quite a long way from the nearest town."

"On a ranch near Pomo?" the woman asked and then added, with some embarrassment, "I couldn't help overhearing you tell the driver you'd be getting off in Pomo. I've lived in Pomo all my life, and I thought I might know—"

"No. It's not really near Pomo. It's closer to Sturmville, actually. But I'm being met in Pomo."

"Near Sturmville? Well, I'm not quite as well acquainted that far north, but I do know a few of the older families. What are their names—the people you'll be visiting?"

"Corey. My father-in-law is—was—Lucien Corey. He died recently."

"Corey?" There was a pause while the woman's eyes flickered to Paul and back again to Beth. "Corey. Yes, I've heard the name. I don't know them personally, but I've heard of—the Coreys." There was a fluttering of hands and a magazine fell into the aisle. As the woman bent to retrieve it, Beth bent too, and lifted it into the plump hand.

"Thanks," a strangely stiffened smile stretched the pink lips and, opening the magazine, the woman turned her attention to its pages. The tables had turned now. Now it was Beth's turn to watch and wait for an opening, to squirm in the grip of curiosity. The woman had said she knew of them—Jon's family—

5

and even if she knew only a little, it would probably be more than Beth knew. There were so many questions that were as yet unanswered—and might go unanswered for a long time to come.

How long would she have to know them before she could ask, "Why did John cut himself off from you so completely? Why did he tell me you were all dead?"

Not that the pink person could answer that, but anything at all would be helpful—if only she'd look up from the magazine. What kind of people are the Coreys? No—too abrupt. Something innocuous at first. How much farther is it to Pomo? How many miles? That should be all right, and only then go on to other things.

Beth stared openly across the aisle, cleared her throat slightly, but there was no response. She considered a more forthright approach—a touch on the arm—a "Pardon me, but. . . ." Considered—but came to no decision.

Decisions, it seemed, did not grow easier with practice. Decisions—huge, threatening decisions—exhausted and immobilized one, especially when they had to be made alone, with no help or warning. Why had there been no warning? Why had Jon told her they were all dead? Why, Jon? Why did you do it?

But that was too close—too close to those other questions about Jon's death—the torturing questions that some fiendish director produced for her edification on the dark screens of midnight awakenings, and at other undefended moments. All right. No more. No more questions. Not even how many miles to Pomo?

6

—or London Town?—or, where are you going my pretty maid?—or, who killed Cock Robin?

She closed her eyes against the pain. Very clever, she told the midnight director. Very clever.

"Umm. Umm." Beth had almost given up trying to get Paul to call her anything else. Opening her eyes, she saw his face, blurred and liquid, very close to her own. "Umm," he said again. "There's Mundy out there running in the grass. I saw him. I think he's coming with us."

Beth swallowed, blinked and managed an unsteady smile. "He is? Mundy? That's—great. I think it's great that Mundy's coming with us." Aware of a certain defensiveness in her tone, she was able to trace it to Ms. Calvert, the nursery school teacher who had warned against encouraging Paul's fantasies. "Not that I'm against imaginary friends. I think it's quite natural actually. But it's just that Paul's are so numerous, and so persistent. So much of the time he seems to be—out of touch with reality" At the time Beth had agreed, uncertainly. But now, with so many changes to be faced, so many differences to be adjusted to, it seemed good to be able to take along one familiar—she couldn't seem to remember just what Mundy was. A horse probably, given Paul's passion for all things equine.

She leaned forward and looked out the window. Beyond a narrow grassy valley floor, the hills were closer now and heavily wooded. Paul was looking too, flattening his nose against the glass. "See him? See Mundy out there?"

"I'm not sure. I think so. Is Mundy a horse, Paul?"

7

"Mostly. Mostly he's a horse. Today he's more of a dragon."

"Of course," Beth said. "Of course I can see him." She put both arms around Paul and hugged him, suddenly grateful for his certainty, and his dragons, and his soft young warmth. Grateful, too, for one of the rare moments, so much rarer since Jonathan's death, when her love for Paul was purely joyful, unsullied by the haunting fears that made her hate herself and motherhood and even, sometimes, Paul himself. For a moment he allowed the hug, but then he pushed her away and was gone, absorbed into the world that he inhabited with serene conviction and the rapt attention of a baby animal. Wide-eyed, bluntnosed, insanely innocent, Paul's stare enchanted and tormented her—the calm, wondering gaze of a lion cub watching a blowing flower, or the approach of the hyena who comes to kill. Once more his strangely beautiful eyes, darkened by enormous irises, were focused on something in the far distance, on something dragonlike that ran beside them over the valley floor.

There had been dragons in Beth's dreams once. Lovely green and gold dragons with transparent wings, and unicorns and giants and mermaids, and handsome princes who would come someday to make everything all right. Good dreams, for the most part, and it had been Bettina, with all her failings as a person and a mother, who had given them form. Even on the bad days when Bettina's eyes were wild, and her beautiful hair drifted around her face tangled as seaweed, she had always read out loud, played games and told stories—the best-loved things over and over again until they became a part of everything. For awhile, before they went to live at Uncle Al's, the world had been Beth and Bettina and Mother Goose, Hans C. Andersen and Aesop and the Blue Fairy and all the rest. The woman across the hall had been Mother Hubbard, the landlord Rumplestiltzskin, the butcher Jack Sprat. Beth had been Miss Muffet or sometimes Wee Willie Winkie, and Bettina had called herself Cinderella. But, secretly, to Beth, she had always been the Little Mermaid—a mermaid with a fragile seashell face, and dark eyes, wet with tears for the prince who had gone away.

Past Paul's head, beyond the window, a herd of black and white cows drifted by, and then a farmhouse fled past, primly square and white in the midst of its following of lesser buildings—groveling garages and sycophant sheds. A rooster scratched in the driveway and, suddenly, she was eight again, and the farm was Uncle Al's. She was back again in the crowded rooms, stifling with unvented gas heat and prayerful resentment, while outside there was always wind and dust and the smell and sound of chickens.

She had dreamed of them again, only the night before. Trying to sleep for the last time in the bleak, stripped apartment, most of their belongings already sold or in storage, she had lain awake for hours listening to Paul's steady breathing from the cot across the room. And when sleep finally came, it brought with it the dream of chickens. Only this time there were many of them instead of two, and they were all dead; slaughtered and plucked and yet, horribly, still alive. Whitely naked, their legs ending in raw stumps, they had hobbled past her, turning cold skinned heads, aware of her presence, although their eyes were only bloody sockets. And she had known that they were pleading and there was nothing she could do. The old litany began again, "No. No. I'm sorry. I'm sorry. I didn't mean . . ."

Clenching her fists, fingernails pressed into palms to enforce the reality of present pain, Beth brought her attention back to the world of the moment, to a small fleeting world enclosed in glass and metal and pervaded by the drone of tires on asphalt. Across the aisle the pink woman still read feverishly.

2

T H E letter had arrived on a Saturday morning almost six weeks before. Mop in hand, Beth had answered the doorbell and signed the release impatiently, certain that the letter was only one more in an endless series of communications from Jonathan's insurance company. She had given up on the insurance long before. She would be only too happy to have Western State Mutual keep their money and stop the endless investigations, the prying and probing that had made it so much harder to forget the past and accept the fact of Jonathan's death. With her mind still occupied with the hectic three-ring circus of a working mother's weekend, she had torn the large envelope open and taken out a fat sheaf of papers. But instead of Western State's familiar logo, the letter-head had announced that she was being communicated with by the law offices of Garfield and Pratt of Pomo, California. Pomo, she thought. I don't know

11

anybody in Pomo. Except for a vague notion that it was in the northern part of the state, she didn't even know where it was. Propping the mop against the doorframe, she had begun to read, and had stayed in the same position for a long, long time, transfixed by astonishment.

At first, Warren had been as dumbfounded as she. Warren Crawford had been a year ahead of Jonathan at UCLA. Beth had known him slightly then, and later she had known that Jonathan considered him a competent lawyer. And she had not blamed him for the loss of the insurance money. The fact that she had, sometime before, resolved not to see him again, had not been related to any professional inadequacies on Warren's part. That something had been inadequate in other aspects of their relationship was certain, but she was not at all sure what it was—or who.

Warren Crawford was, Beth had discovered, a tireless experimenter in the field of beautiful relationships, with a decided emphasis on variety and dispatch. When she had come to him about the insurance, a new widow, lost and lonely, he had undoubtedly considered her a sure thing. And she had been—but not for long. Just as the legal talents of Warren Crawford, attorney, had been futile against the evidence compiled by the insurance company, the romantic expertise of Warren Crawford, practitioner in the field of beautiful relationships, had been ineffective against Beth's malady. Not that she hadn't found his opening moves to be flattering and even, for a while, distracting. But all too soon it became apparent that Warren's offering, physical and tangible though it undoubtedly was, became nebulous and unreal when weighed against the overwhelming presence of her continuing pain.

She had enjoyed his company and been grateful for his interest, but their lovemaking had been marred, for her at least—if Warren had been dissatisfied he hadn't said so—by a strange feeling of disassociation. In bed with Warren she had found herself strangely detached, possessed of the dreamer's ability to be both participant and observer, a condition that evoked a voyeuristic titillation that had not been unexciting, but that had left a residue of deep anxiety—and loss. When she called a halt, Warren had been surprised and perhaps a little shaken. She had, however, felt sure that it had not been the ending of their relationship that he found so upsetting. Warren, she felt sure, was good at endings. It was more that he was not accustomed to endings that he hadn't initiated. But for whatever reasons, he had shown himself to be wounded. So it was that Beth had arrived at his office with the documents from Garfield and Pratt, feeling uncertain of her reception and, irrationally, a little bit guilty.

Warren's greeting, however, had been warmly enthusiastic, with only the slightest tinge of soulfulness to suggest the injured party. But when he had finished skimming through the sheaf of papers, any recrimination that he might have had in mind was forgotten, swept away by astonishment and what seemed to be real delight.

"My God, Beth. Do you realize what this means—to Paul's future, not to mention your own?"

Paul's future. They had planned, she and Jonathan, for Paul's future to include all the good things, open pathways towards whatever destiny he might choose. And Warren had known how crucial the insurance money had been to her hopes of fulfilling such plans, a widow with no resources and little earning potential. And now Warren's delight seemed so genuine, untouched by professional interests, as lawyer or lover, that for a moment she was sorry she had ended the relationship, or at least that she had done it so abruptly. She could have been kinder, allowing him time enough to convince himself that the parting had been his idea, or at least a mutual agreement.

Warren's attention had gone back to the papers. He was leafing through them again, shaking his head in disbelief. "That much acreage, and a lot of it near the coast. I don't know much about land values in that area but there seems to be a lot of timber land and a sawmill as well as the sheep. One hell of a lot of sheep. It looks to me like you're the mother of a millionaire or very close to it." The delighted grin faded as he shook his head incredulously. "You really knew nothing of this possibility? Wait a minute, I remember now. You said that Jonathan had no living relatives."

"That's what I always thought. At least—" She paused and then decided to go on. "—At least, that's what I'd thought for nine years, since before we were married. But lately, since this happened, I have remembered something. When we first met, we'd been talking about backgrounds, the way you do when you first meet, and Jon said, or I think he did, that he

14

grew up in northern California and that his family still lived there. But later, when we began to get really involved, I mentioned his parents and he said they were dead. He said I must have misunderstood before. He never would talk very much about his childhood. He said that his parents had been strange people and that his childhood hadn't been particularly happy, and he just didn't enjoy talking about it—that it depressed him."

"And you let it go at that? You weren't curious enough to press him?"

"I tried to, of course, from time to time. But—well, you knew Jonathan. You couldn't press him. People just didn't."

"Yes. I suppose that's true. Well, if we'd had any idea about the possibility of something like this happening, I wouldn't have felt quite so bad about losing the suit. It certainly seems as if your worries about Paul's future are over."

"I—I don't know."

Warren looked at her intently, his face sobering. Putting down the stack of documents, he patted them into a neat pile and pushed them aside. Leaning forward, he gave her his full attention.

"It occurs to me," he said at last, "that you are singularly unenthused about what would appear, to your average materialistic neighborhood attorney, to be an incredible stroke of luck. What's the matter, Beth? I'd like to think that it's the part about having to live on the property that's bothering you. As in— having to move away and leave behind someone who's very important to you, namely me. But my better

15

judgment tells me that's not it. What is it that's bothering you?"

"I don't know," she repeated. "It's nothing—that is, it's not logical. I suppose it's just that I'd thought of them as dead for so long. And now to find that they're alive—so many of them. His mother and his grandmother, and his father too, until a few weeks ago. Why would he do such a thing, Warren? Not to see them for all that time? Even to say they were all dead?"

"You realize, of course, that he may have been in touch with them without your knowing it. Obviously they knew about you, and about Paul."

"I don't know. I suppose it's possible."

"But it does seem very strange that he didn't tell you more about it—about what it was he had against them. You'd think he'd at least have blamed some personal defect on the way they'd warped him. If he never used that one from time to time, he must have been the only member of our generation who didn't."

"No. He really didn't, at least not to me. He almost never mentioned them at all, except when I would ask, and then it was just—well, very factual information. Very unemotional. Like the fact that his grandfather was from Massachusetts. And he did tell me that his family had a sheep ranch, but I got the impression that it was very small. Certainly nothing like"—she gestured toward the sheaf of papers—"that. I thought he must have used up any money they'd left him while he was still an undergraduate. Oh, I do remember one comment he made about his father. I'd said something about how good-looking he was—Jonathan, I mean—and he said I should have

16

seen his father. He said that compared to his father, he was a real also-ran."

"Yeah? God. The old man must have been a hot item with the local ladies."

"Hmm," Beth nodded. "He said something to that effect. Something about suspecting that he had a lot of half brothers and sisters scattered around northern California."

"What did he say about his mother?"

"Not much. He talked about her less than the others. But I think he must have cared about her, at least at one time. He told me once that she had taught him the names of trees and flowers, things like that. And there was something about the way he said it that made me think he'd cared about her."

"Did he tell you how they happened to die—what became of them?"

"Yes he did. But obviously it wasn't true. Except, maybe about his grandfather. He said his grandfather died of a heart attack a long time ago—before Jon left home—and I guess that may have been true. But he said that his father was shot in a hunting accident—and that wasn't true, obviously."

"And his mother?"

"Of a stroke, I think it was. And he never mentioned the aunt, Eva Weber, or any of her family. I'm positive he never said anything about her at all."

"Anything else?"

"Not really. Except . . ."

"Except?"

"There was something once. I'd almost forgotten about it. It was about a picture, an old photo portrait of a man. I bought it at an antique show, for the

17

frame mostly. But I really was intrigued by the old man. He was lean and stern, with a kind of fierceness about him. I hung him up in the hall, just until I could find the right picture for the frame. And one day when I came home from work he was gone. Jon had thrown him out. Torn him up, I suppose. I never saw him again. The frame was just hanging there, empty. When I asked Jon about it, he said the picture depressed him—because it reminded him of his grandfather. I did press him a little that time. I said I hated it when he was so secretive, that it made me feel shut out—you know, excluded. But he wouldn't say anymore, and after awhile he got angry and I stopped asking."

Warren had gotten up then and, coming around the desk to where she was sitting, he took both her hands and led her to the couch. Sitting beside her, he held her hands and let his eyes—vivid blue eyes that he used to great advantage in the cultivation of beautiful relationships—say that she had his full attention and care and concern. It was a thing that he did very well. But somehow, on that day, she had wanted, needed so much to believe in the caring, that she wasn't aware of techniques and mechanics, as she so often was with Warren.

"Beth," he said. "You've never talked to me about Jonathan except for the things I had to know because they concerned the—accident."

Warren had always been good about that—even now, since the court rulings and the insurance company's decision, he still called it "the accident." Just once, a long time ago, before all the investigations, he

18

had asked Beth if there was any chance, even the slightest possibility, that it might have been suicide. She couldn't remember what she had said—or did— but apparently she had convinced him of something—if only that he mustn't ask her that question. Someday she'd go over it again with him—how it had to have been an accident—how Jon could have opened the gate and driven through the field to the edge of the cliff because he was tired and tense and the sight of the ocean always helped him—calmed him. And then, at the edge, there'd been some kind of mistake, or he had gone to sleep, forgetting to set the brakes, but not now, not yet. She wasn't ready yet to talk about it.

"I know that your relationship was very important to you both," Warren had gone on; "but Jon has been dead now for almost two years, and it seems to me that you haven't let go of him. You really haven't started to forget the past and begin living for yourself, and Paul. Why don't you tell me about Jonathan and your marriage? Maybe it would help to talk about it."

Beth had felt herself stiffening. "You knew him. You know what he was like."

"Not really. I only knew him at school, as a casual friend. And he was married and I wasn't, so we weren't on the same social trip. I liked him, when I wasn't envying him his goddamn—I don't know what to call it—charisma, I guess—but that doesn't cover it. He charmed people all right, but it was more than that, except perhaps in the sense that a snake charmer charms a snake. I mean, he could really pull fangs,

19

psychically speaking. You know, turn cobras into out-size angle worms. I'll never forget the way he handled old Hubbell. You remember Hubbell?"

"Yes, I think so. Wasn't he the one who wrote all those books on criminal law?"

"Right. That old bastard had the rest of us completely tyrannized, but not Corey. In fact, it almost seemed to be the other way around. I remember thinking that Corey really had it made. On his way to becoming a real pistol of a trial lawyer, and with a beautiful wife to support him until he could start raking it in." Warren had paused, smiling ruefully. "I remember kidding him once about that presence of his. About the way he could take over a situation, or a roomful of people. I mean, it was like mesmerization. I told him it was going to be a great asset in the courtroom. I meant it as a compliment, but I don't think he took it that way. He just stared at me and stalked off."

"Yes," Beth said, "Jonathan was . . ." She had stopped and said nothing for a long time. To say that he had been the center of her existence would be trite—and misleading. A center implies surrounding territory, an area beyond, and there had been none. Nothing beyond Jonathan. She thought of the word enchantment—and then, obsession. In the end she only shook her head. "I can't now. I'll talk about him sometime. But I can't now."

"Okay." He had patted her shoulder. "Some other time. But there is this other small matter of your son's inheritance." He got up briskly, exasperated or perhaps hurt, and going to his desk brought back the sheaf of papers. "What are you going to do about it?

It looks to me as if the decision is going to have to be all yours."

"I know. That's what frightens me. I want—I think I really want to say no. We'd have to go there and live with all those people. In the same house, perhaps, or at least on the property. Who knows what they'll be like. His mother and grandmother and apparently his aunt and her family live on the property, too. And we'll have to stay there, at least enough of the time to make it our legal residence, until Paul is twenty-one. It really frightens me. But on the other hand, if I refuse, Paul may hate me for it someday. I just don't know what to do."

"But your decision wouldn't be irrevocable, you know. If you accept, for Paul, and go there to live and then find that it really isn't worth it, that the situation is bad enough to outweigh the value of the inheritance, you could always change your mind and leave."

"I suppose so, but it wouldn't be easy. To come back and start over with no job or place to live."

"You could store your things for awhile until you see how it goes. And it seems you and Paul will be receiving a fourth of the net income from the property up until the time when he is to inherit outright, on his twenty-first birthday. There's no indication of just what that would be, but it should be a substantial amount. It shouldn't be too hard for you to save up a little nest egg. Enough to tide you over if you decide to give it all up and return to honorable poverty."

"I suppose you're right."

"I don't know whether I am nor not. And I certainly don't want to influence your decision. For one thing, I'm going to hate to see you go, even though, in a manner of speaking, you already have. At least as far as our relationship is concerned."

"Warren, I . . ."

"It's all right. That decision was yours to make, too. It's just that I can still hope as long as you're around. But as far as the other thing goes, this inheritance, all I can do is to be sure you're aware of all the legal aspects, provisions, contingencies, and so on. After that—it's all up to you, Beth."

Please, please stop saying that, she had thought. I know I'll have to decide, but how can I when I don't know, really, what it is I'm deciding, or why, or what my decision will do to us, to Paul and me. It still amazed her to think that she had, in fact, decided. There had been so many things to consider. She had tried to think only of Paul, of Paul's welfare, Paul's future, but she had had to acknowledge other motivations, other temptations. She found herself to be tempted by the possibility of some measure of leisure for herself. She had worked since she was fifteen—weekends, vacations, after school, until she had graduated from UCLA, and full time since, except for six months when Paul was born. She had never liked her job. In school she had dreamed of writing, had planned to teach, and had settled for office work as a temporary expedient until Jon finished school and established a practice. The time had almost come, she had set a date for quitting work and was trying to decide whether to go back to school or take time out to try writing again, when Jon died—and she had gone on working—and on—and on.

There had never been any choice—with Jon's insurance nullified and with the debts from his last years of law school still unpaid. The debts had been like a dark cloud, heavy and endless, until at some point in her deliberations the realization came that if she sold her car and furniture and used the last of her meager savings, she could pay them all off—be rid of them once and for all. Of course, she would be left with barely enough money for bus tickets to Pomo, but they could arrive free and clear of old burdens, ready to begin a new life.

There had been other temptations, too—vague and unexpected yearnings. She had discovered that there was something strongly appealing about the thought of being a part of a family, a family of many generations, deeply rooted in time and place. The fact that she could identify the yearning as a residue of her own rootless and transient childhood made it no less seductive.

There was a fascination, too, in the thought that she would be living among Jonathan's people. The attraction here was less rational. Did she think that Jonathan would seem closer there? Or was it, perhaps, only the need to know. To seek there, where his life began, for clues that might help her to understand its ending.

There were, on the other hand, equally vague and unreasonable fears. Most of them were irrational, unjustifiable, dim foreboding shadows, except for the one justly frightening fact—that Jonathan had renounced his family, had denied their very existence. Over and over again she had asked herself what could have happened between them to cause so complete and irreconcilable a rift.

The break must have come when he was quite

young. He had been twenty-four and in his first year of law school when they had met, and she knew he had already been living in Southern California for several years by then. They had met at a party given by mutual friends. In the small, crowded room his presence had been a magnetic force. She had been hypnotized, breathless. But he'll never notice me, she'd thought, never want me. When he'd first spoken to her, she'd known that her eyes were offering more than she'd meant them to, more than she'd thought possible. She had been sure that he would be turned off, bored by such instant surrender. But miraculously he hadn't been. She hadn't bored him, and he had never bored her. There had been times later when he thwarted, frustrated, even frightened her, but he had never failed to hold her complete attention, command her unconditional response. His presence had been an enclosing force that anchored her being in time and space, stilled her old demons, and absorbed her into an enchanted bondage through which she had moved like a sleepwalker for almost seven years. To remember, to evoke his presence, opened the lid of a forbidden coffer and memories swarmed out; vivid sensate memories, but dangerously fragile. And just beyond, the stalking, punishing pain.

"Look, Umm. We're stopping. Are we almost there? Can we see it?"

Paul's nose was pressed against the window. The landscape had changed again. The trees were closer now, crowding the roadside. Among them, here and there, were clearings occupied by buildings, houses and small shabby commercial buildings—a restaurant, a service station, the unlovely overlapping fringe of town and country that heralds the approach of a small town. Across the aisle the pink woman was bustling, tucking her magazine into a crowded shopping bag, shouldering her purse, her eyes turned carefully away from Beth and Paul.

"I think we're coming into Pomo," Beth said. "We can't see the ranch yet. We still have a long way to go by car."

"But we can almost see it, can't we? Can we almost see it, Umm?"

"Yes, almost." Beth told him.

3

T H E bus station, like all places of passage, had a barren, breathless quality, unquickened and souless. Caged within the grimy sterility of its enameled walls, even Paul seemed cut off from his gift for the present, unable to find a fascination with which to celebrate the moment. Cuddling against Beth, he begged to go. "Let's go, Umm. Let's go to the Farm." And at the next minute, "Let's go home. I want to go back home."

They had waited for almost an hour. Beth had checked at the ticket counter for a message and had tried phoning, only to discover that the Corey phone, if there was one, was unlisted. Having been told only that she would be met, she had been regarding every new arrival with hopeful interest. Her impatience was beginning to turn into real anxiety when a man burst through the doorway and paused to survey the room.

Thick-bodied, of middle age and height, he seemed enitrely nondescript, except for his prominent pale blue eyes, but he was obviously looking for someone, and that made him the likeliest prospect to enter in some time. The pale eyes fell on Beth and Paul, the man started forward, and Beth's hopefulness turned to apprehension. The man was drunk.

Listing heavily, he moved forward, and in a painfully harsh whisper that made Beth look around to see who might be threatening to listen, announced himself as Matthew Weber, Jonathan's uncle by marriage. Looking carefully at Beth's shoes, in what appeared to be a nervous inability to meet her eyes, he explained that he was sorry to be late, but that he had had several errands to attend to, and they had taken longer than he had expected. It seemed obvious that one of the errands had been accomplished in a local bar. But as Weber collected Beth's luggage, it became apparent that he was not as drunk as she had feared. It was true that his breath smelled of liquor, but the listing gait was probably due to an injury or deformity rather than intoxication. Outside the station he lurched towards a large, rugged van.

A few miles outside of Pomo, Beth discovered an alarming problem and shortly afterwards its solution. Left to his own devices, Matthew Weber seemed more interested in examining his passengers than in keeping the van on the right side of the road. A moment's silence and his eyes began to flicker to the right, and the van began to drift, frighteningly, off its course. But having already established his inability to look directly at anyone he was actually talking to, the solution was obvious. All that was necessary was to keep him talking. In avoiding her gaze, he would be forced, she hoped, to give some attention to the road ahead. So for a long exhausting hour she asked questions feverishly, and Weber answered, sometimes with garrulous enthusiasm and at others with strangely ambiguous equivocations. But Beth's interest in one answer in particular was totally sincere.

"Where will Paul and I be living?" As she asked the question, she was suddenly seized by a shiver of apprehension. It was a question she had asked before by mail, and Garfield and Pratt had answered that adequate and private living quarters would be provided on the property. But in the one letter she had received from a family member, a cordial but brief typewritten note from Margaret Corey, no mention of living arrangements had been made.

"Why, in the house," Weber answered.

"In the house? Is there only one?"

He laughed. "No need for more. There's plenty of room. They're giving you Lucien and Rachel's wing. No one's been using it lately. Plenty of room."

Beth's heart sank. "The lawyers spoke of private quarters," she said.

The pale eyes flickered. "Private?" Weber grinned. "Oh well, this'll be private enough. Your own kitchen and all. Like a separate house except under one roof. The old man liked to keep everything under one roof." A chuckle and again the flickering eyes. On Beth's lap Paul watched, head tilted, and then chuckled in imitation. Paul was a natural mimic and usually an amazingly accurate one, but the grimace that on the man's face had seemed only meaningless and unwarranted, transposed onto Paul's became vaguely obscene—a leering cherub. Involuntarily Beth put her hand over his face. When he pulled it away, the leer was gone leaving only the familiar cheerful bemusement of Paul's smile.

"By the old man, do you mean Lucien?" Beth asked.

"Lucien," Weber snorted. "No, not hardly. Guess Jonathan never told you much about his family. That right?"

"Not very much."

There was another attack of snorting chuckles accompanied by knowing nods before Weber said, "Well, it's not for me to fill you in on any details, not being properly a Corey myself, but I can set you straight on a few facts, I guess. The old man was Calvin. Calvin Corey." He drew out the name with a flourish like a public introduction. "Came to California back in 1909 and married Margaret O'Donnell Bradley. Been dead almost twenty years now."

"Calvin, you mean?" Beth asked. "Margaret is still alive, isn't she?"

"That's right. She was a good bit younger than Calvin, but she's getting on now, too. Eighty-two, she is and not what she used to be. Not by a long shot." Again the suggestive laugh, and then, "Two children, Calvin and Margaret had. Just the two, Lucien and Eva, right close together." The road was climbing sharply and Weber busied himself with the gears. "Right close"—he shifted down busily, tromping on the clutch—"together. Lucien was . . ." Again a long pause for a virtuoso performance on clutch and

29

gear shift during which he seemed to have lost the thread of his narration.

"And Lucien and Rachel were Jonathan's parents," Beth prompted.

"Right. Right you are. Lucien and Rachel were Jonathan's parents, but you might say he was the old man's idea, Jonathan was. Lucien wasn't what you might call the marrying kind, but Calvin was real concerned about an heir, so he kind of picked Rachel out for Lucien. Then I came along. Not long after Jonathan was born I happened by the Farm one day with a load of hardware"—another long, chuckling pause—"and the first thing you know I was a married man. And a father. Two boys. You hear about our boys? Eva's and mine?"

"Yes. That is, I heard there were two—cousins of Jonathan's."

"That's right. Two of them." This time there was something so pointedly insinuating in the flickering glance that Beth wondered if Weber meant to imply something about the inheritance—to hint that there were other descendants who had rightful claims to Corey property. But if that were his meaning, he declined to elaborate, or even to offer any further information about the family. Apparently deciding that he had said enough, his responses to Beth's questions became briefer and more confusing. Not so much uninformative as ambiguous, as if the simple surface statements had other meanings. She soon decided that less personal questions were best to keep him droning on—and watching the road. Questions about the Sturmville area, its history, climate, and industry, brought long rambling answers, leaving her free to think of other things. To think despairingly at one moment that she had made a terrible mistake, and at the next to remind herself that Matthew Weber, strange as he might be, was only one member of the family, and not necessarily representative. Not even properly a Corey, as he himself had pointed out.

"When did the Webers come to this area?" she asked hastily during a lull that sent the pale eyes sliding in her direction and the van drifting towards the shoulder.

"Ninety-five. My grandpa came out to Sacramento and bought a wagon and goods and headed north. Tradespeople they were, not farmers. The Webers have always been townspeople. Not like the Coreys. Now you take old man Corey. The land was in his blood like a fever. They're all that way, the Coreys. But my grandpa, all he wanted was just a city lot and enough lumber to put up a general store, and within ten years he'd built up the best line of merchandise in a hundred miles."

"How did your grandfather happen to pick Sturmville?"

"He didn't. Not in ninety-five. Weren't nothing in Sturmville in ninety-five but a tannery run by an old man named Sturm. The town was called Bradley then, and it was quite a bit farther down the valley on a real pretty little meadow. It's all part of the Corey property now. It was my father who moved the store to Sturmville after the fire in nineteen eighteen."

"The store burned down?"

Again the strange inappropriate laugh. "The whole town burned. Not to mention a lot of livestock and five or six citizens who didn't run fast enough for one

31

reason or another. Wasn't running too fast myself at the time, being only about a year old. But I was one of the lucky ones. Only got singed a bit."

Thrusting out his right arm, Weber turned it to expose a narrow strip of puckered discolored skin that widened as it disappeared beneath the rolled sleeve of his shirt. Beth struggled to keep from shrinking visibly from the outthrust arm, but Paul was leaning forward, studying the scar with great interest.

The arm was finally removed and for a moment Weber drove in silence, his eyes on the road. Paul was still staring, but at the man's face, now. When he turned back to Beth, his round brow was puckered.

"I didn't do it?" he said. "Did I, Umm?"

"Do what? What didn't you do?"

"Hurt him? I didn't hurt his arm?"

"Of course not, Paul. What a funny thing to ask."

Paul nodded, but his eyes were clouded. Putting his thumb in his mouth he cuddled against Beth, pulling up his knees. He rarely sucked his thumb anymore. Weber was chuckling again, and Beth found herself struggling against a dark wave of dismay. She knew she shouldn't have agreed to come. She had only been fooling herself about doing it for Paul. There were other reasons, selfish reasons, and if it all turned out to be a horrible mistake. . . .

"Well, there it is. The city of Sturmville," Weber said, and she found that a curve in the road had made visible before and below them a narrow valley floor. Thick growths of evergreens covered the surrounding hills and marched out across the valley to where the highway was briefly bordered by a straggle of buildings. A few more steeply descending curves and the van swept by a shabby Quonset-type building presiding over a gathering of obviously ailing cars and trucks. Then came a bar with a log cabin facade, a large modern grocery store, a small department store, and up ahead the buildings were already thinning towards the end of town.

"Not much of a place after Los Angeles," Weber said. "Expect you're going to miss . . ." Breaking off, he pointed to the left. "There. That old building on the left, where it says hardware. That was my father's store. Belongs to a family named Garvey now. Not much of a place anymore. Now me, I'd like to own a store right in the middle of a big city. Like Los Angeles. Now there's a real city."

"Well, it has it faults. Have you been there lately?"

"Me? To Los Angeles?" He looked at Beth sharply and then quickly away. "To Los Angeles lately? No, not lately. A long time ago. Must have been over ten years ago. Haven't been there lately."

The road was narrow now and curving, winding through heavily wooded foothills. The sky was reddening in the west, and over the eastern hills it had faded to a clear colorless luminosity. At last Weber said, "Only about five miles now. Used to drive this road in a Model T when I worked for my father, making deliveries. Carried supplies out to the lumbering camps, mostly. Lots of money being made in lumber in those days." The voice rambled on, the road climbed steadily, and the sun had just disappeared, when Weber's tone quickened. "All this is Corey land now. Starts right here at the road." And a moment later, "There she is, on that ridge up ahead. the Farmhouse."

4

S E E N from the road the Farmhouse barely topped
the rise, its chimneys, gables, and cupolas forming a
dark fringe against the sunset sky. The van stopped
before a rusty wrought-iron gate while Weber struggled with an enormous padlock, and then zigzagged
upwards in a series of sharp cutbacks. As they wound
their way up, the house seemed to grow out of the
cleft in the hills, looming taller and then branching
out into wings and projections, under a roof that
angled and slanted in a profusion of sloping surfaces.
Dodging Paul's bobbing head, Beth watched with
amazed fascination as the house grew and prolifer-
ated across the slope and down into the draw.

"Surprises you, don't it?" Weber said.

"It's—huge. It seemed much smaller from the
road."

"Like I told you, it's big—and old. Parts of it's

older than others. The old man just kept tacking wings onto it."

"That part you see from the road, that tallest section, is that a part of the original house? The style seems different. More Victorian."

"That's right. That was the old O'Donnell house. Been there a long time. Way before the old man got ahold of it."

A final steep climb and the van entered a rutted drive that circled a spreading oak tree and came to a stop before a curving veranda. Above the veranda the house towered to a third story and a jumble of gables and dormers, an unrestrained gingerbread orgy. But to the south the wing that extended down the slope seemed, in contrast, primly utilitarian, a graft from a colonial saltbox. It was another wing, however, that caught and held Beth's attention. Extending from the original house at right angles, this section was massively built, faced with rough native stone—and clearly abandoned. The lower windows were heavily boarded over and the upper ones dark and empty. As Matthew Weber and the house waited, Beth and Paul on her lap sat very still, staring.

There was something in that first moment like a fleeting sense of recognition. As if something had struggled briefly upwards, and then sunk back again into the dark obscurity from which the only escape is by dream. Beth had always dreamed houses. Houses she had once inhabited, or visited, houses she had seen in films or only read about, appeared regularly in vividly realistic dreams, so clearly imaged that she often awoke remembering exact floor plans and details of furnishings. But there were other dreams that concerned less sane and reasonable houses; strangely fluid houses that grew and changed before her eyes, hallways that beckoned and then grew endlessly beneath her feet, ceilingless rooms clustered beneath huge hovering rooftrees, crumbling shacks with palatial interiors. She inhabited such dreams anxiously, involved always in some vague search for a forgotten secret or neglected duty, or for the fulfillment of some tantalizingly uncertain expectation. But with the anxiety there was always a seductive fascination that made her awake reluctantly, reaching backwards into the thickening darkness, just as she was now reaching eagerly forward towards the incredible structure that sprawled along the crest of the saddleback between two wooded peaks. Afterwards, remembering that first moment, she could not be certain if it had been then, or only later looking back, that there had seemed to be something else—something beyond her own reaction. As if somewhere in that great sprawling hulk something had stirred, reaching out and summoning them into the shelter of its walls.

"Well, here we are," Weber was saying. "Everybody out."

Beth opened the door. "Here we are, Paul. Jump down. We're at the Farm." But Paul's eagerness to arrive at their new home had suddenly dissipated, and turning he clung to Beth's neck, forcing her to struggle out of the cab burdened by the weight of his small sturdy body. She was still trying to disengage the clinging fingers from around her neck when someone spoke to her from the veranda.

A tall, well-formed woman was standing in the door. She was wearing a jeans suit and a man's shirt that strained over her full breasts, and her abundant gray hair was pulled back and tied at the nape of her neck. As Beth came up the steps, she hurried forward, extending her hands. "Eva Weber. Eva Corey Weber." And then, turning to her husband who was struggling up the steps with the luggage, "We were worried, Matthew. Was the bus late?"

"The bus. Well, yes, the bus . . ." The momentum of his erratic charge up the stairs carried him into the doorway, forcing his wife to retreat before him into the hall, where the hollow of the house swallowed the whispery rasp of his voice. So if the bus got the blame, Beth didn't hear it, but in any case she had ceased to listen. Over Matthew's shoulder she was staring at Eva's face. Set in the fine-boned angular face of a middle-aged woman were familiar eyes. Like Jonathan's, Eva Weber's eyes were large, well set, and darkly lashed, but it was more than that. As Eva's eyes had met hers, Beth had been aware of a deeply centered force—the same strange aura of inner strength that had made it so easy for Jonathan to charm, or intimidate.

The inevitable pain that lay in wait for any opening surged up, mingling strangely with an unexpected hungry joy. Dazedly she answered questions. Yes, this was Paul. Yes, the trip had been interesting but, yes they were very tired. Inside a large dimly lit entry hall, Matthew was struggling up a steep stairway that curved towards an enormously high ceiling. But Eva stopped, and taking Paul by both shoulders, she went down on one knee and looked at him.

37

Looked, and went on looking, while Paul, with uncharacteristic patience, stood quietly, wide-eyed, and returned her gaze.

"Like Jonathan," she said at last. "But like Rachel, too. The eyes, I think. But clearly a Corey. Very much a Corey." She released him then and stood up, but her eyes still followed him. Followed him as she spoke to Beth, as they went up the stairs and along hallways.

Still in a kind of sensory paralysis brought on partly perhaps by exhaustion but also by the shock of Eva's eyes, Beth was aware only dimly of darkly paneled walls hung with pictures and mirrors. Another hallway narrower and even more shadowy, ended at an arched doorway, beyond which a short flight of stairs led at an angle to a lower level.

"We're in the northeast wing now," Eva said. "It was Lucien and Rachel's. Jonathan grew up here. But Rachel moved into the old house with Margaret after Lucien died. It's been closed up since then. Smells a bit stuffy, I'm afraid."

A sudden thought chilled. "Is the lower floor boarded up?"

"Boarded up? Oh no. You're thinking of the wing that you saw from the front drive? On your left? That's to the west, and almost perpendicular to this section. I don't wonder that you're turned around. It's a very confusing house, I'm afraid."

Ahead of them, Matthew put down the bags, opened a door, and trudged back past them without speaking. "Oma tidied up this corner bedroom," Eva said, "but there are two others in this wing and later on you can take your pick. The bath is just across the hall. There's a kitchen downstairs and a small sitting room, but we'll be expecting you for meals in the old house, at least for awhile, until you've had a chance to rest a bit and settle in. I could show you around a bit more now, but I expect you'd rather have a little time to rest and freshen up before dinner."

"Yes, I think that would be best."

Putting her hand on Beth's shoulder, Eva smiled, and again there was a faint echo, painful and yet fascinating. The mouth was familiar, the lips full and finely edged, the smile quick and intensely personal. "This has been hard for you, I know. Leaving your home—facing the unknown. But now that we've met, I feel certain that things will be fine. Everything is going to be fine for everyone concerned."

Beth felt herself overreacting. Flushing as if in response to an unearned compliment, she struggled against an urge to sigh deeply, as if with relief, or release from anxiety.

"Umm." Paul was tugging at her hand. "Umm, is that my gramma?"

Eva's attention shifted, and Beth was released from the grip on her shoulder—and the smile. "No. This is your aunt. Your Aunt Eva."

"Great aunt, actually. But your grandmother is here. You'll see her very soon."

"Will she be glad to see me?"

"Of course she will. She'll be very glad to see you."

Paul was staring again, his baby-lion stare—pure unblinking wonderment, animallike in its lack of self-consciousness. It was that stare, among other things, that made people wonder about Paul's normality. Taking his shoulders, Beth turned him towards her,

39

forcing a break in his concentration. "We'll see your grandmother soon, and your great grandmother. But right now we're going to unpack and rest awhile."

"I'll run along then," Eva said. "Dinner will be in about an hour. Just follow the hall back the way we came and turn left at the foot of the stairs in the old house."

The room was pleasant, crosslit by two long, narrow lace-curtained windows. Simple and uncluttered, it seemed more New England farmhouse than Victorian mansion. The bed was wrought iron, the rug a braided oval. There were palely twining roses on the walls, and the dresser would have set an antique collector wild with acquisitiveness. Against the far wall there was a small second bed, obviously handmade and beautifully crafted. How many children had slept there, Corey and O'Donnell children, Paul's ancestors. She liked the thought.

On one side of the room the windows looked out on open hillside, a golden grassy slope intersected by a wooded ravine, but the eastern window faced an enormous flagstoned patio that ran the full length of the Victorian section of the house. Enclosed on three sides, it looked inviting, pleasantly sheltered. Near the center was a rocky mound where water trickled from a grottolike formation into an irregularly shaped pond of natural stone. Beyond the pond a single slender tree was encircled by a stone bench, and all along the walls huge redwood planters held flowering shrubs. Between the patio and the house proper there was what seemed to be an enormous conservatory or greenhouse.

The greenhouse at Covenant Farm was amazing,

magically unexpected—the Ice Princess's Palace or the slippery Glass Mountain. Extending along the entire length of the old house, it was similar in its elaborate ornamentation. Thousands of panes of glass, diamonds, rectangles, hexagons, formed the glittering walls and mounted up to a climax of three incredible domes; the two smaller ones, curved and bulbous, and the third, in the center, a towering glass pyramid, encircled by a series of spiky wrought-iron crowns. The interior of the glass palace was invisible, the old panes dulled by time and filmed by moisture were more opaque than transparent, but here and there blurred moss-colored shapes formed twisted patterns against the glass, and in the dim light of early evening the whole structure seemed to pulsate with a dull greenish glow.

"Come look, Paul. Look at this," Beth said, but there was no answer and she turned to find Paul sitting on the edge of the small bed, blank-eyed, rapt in thought.

"Umm," he said suddenly, "is my father here? In this house?"

The sharp twist of pain was followed this time by anger. "Paul," she said sharply, "you know about your father. I've told you and told you. Why do you ask questions like that?"

His eyes were wide, innocent. "I don't know. It just seemed like somebody was. Didn't it. Didn't you? Didn't you, Umm?"

My poor baby, she thought. You've got to stop talking like that before you start school. You've got to learn to be more—ordinary. Out loud she only said, "Come on, Paul. Help me unpack our clothes."

41

5

S H E slept without dreaming and woke at dawn. The face of her watch was clearly visible in the pale misty light. Frowning she put it to her ear. Was dawn earlier here than in Los Angeles, almost six hundred miles to the south? Across the room Paul was still asleep, a small lump under the handsewn quilt, appliquéd with faded rabbits. The air was cool and tinged with woodsy smells, and the silence was almost a sound in itself, pure and deep and soothing. Breakfast at seven thirty was still a long time away. She sank back into warmth and drowsy reverie.

It really seemed she had not dreamed at all, or if she had she remembered nothing, which almost amounted to the same thing. She was usually a prolific and explicit dreamer. Mr. Freeman, the psychologist to whom she had been sent during her first year of college when her health and other aspects of her being seemed on the point of disintegration, had congratulated her on her remarkably transparent dreams. "Your subconscious is admirably straight-forward, Beth. One doesn't have to have done very extensive research in dream analysis to know why you dream about missing the bus that would take you to your dying mother, or why the dream about the chickens is so terrifying. You dream relatively openly about the things that are troubling you. That takes us a giant step in the right direction. Of course there are other steps that need to be taken, and we'll hope that one of them will bring us to where we can see why it is that you insist on feeling responsible for everything that's gone wrong in the universe for the last eighteen years. Once we get to that point, we should be well on our way to home base."

As far as she could tell, she'd never made it to home base, or even close enough to figure out what it might be like, but Mr. Freeman's explorations had been helpful, as had some other discoveries she'd made more or less unassisted. By her sophomore year she'd begun to discover her own mind and body and some of the uses to which they could be put. Under the guidance of a professor dedicated to picking locks on closed minds, she'd gained enough courage to admit doubt and with it came a marvelous overflow-ing of pent-up curiosity. She'd read avidly, argued obnoxiously, and experimented briefly but whole-heartedly with political radicalism, Zen Buddhism, Scientology, and a couple of rather too premeditated love affairs. The overall effect had been at least mildly therapeutic. She'd emerged from each enthusiasm without having done her psyche any apparent damage, but without, on the other hand, having done it a whole lot of good. She'd stopped having crying jags and spells of vomiting, but the nightmares had gone on unabated—until she met Jon. They had subsided dramatically then, and returned after his death, and during the last few weeks they had been at full tide, an exhaustingly constant accompaniment to any lowering of the guards of consciousness. But last night, her first at Covenant Farm, she had come back to her room, put Paul to bed, written a long letter to Warren, and gone to sleep. And the night had contained no panicky awakenings followed by long periods of anxious wakefulness. Something had had a decidedly calming effect on her demons. The long letter to Warren could have played a part—writing had been helpful before. Or it could have been Covenant Farm itself.

It's better and worse than we anticipated. You did ask to hear all about it, so—in order of appearance: We were met in Pomo an hour late by Matthew Weber, the husband of Jonathan's aunt. Matthew is decidedly a minus. There's something almost disgusting about him, but I can't tell you just exactly what. He must be over sixty, average looking except for rather bulgy eyes and a strange tilted limp. But none of that is what matters. It's something much less tangible, I'm sure. I think it's related to a kind of furtive watchfulness. It's as if he looks at everything through some kind of portable psychic keyhole.

44

The trip to Pomo took over an hour and we arrived at Covenant Farm at sunset. The house is really incredible. It stands at the top and down one side of a low saddle in a ridge of hills. The oldest part, the main house, is three stories high, but there are all kinds of wings and extensions of various heights and shapes and sizes, and styles of architecture. It's surrounded by natural growth, almost untended, shrubs and bushes and one tree, a wide, squatty oak, low and spreading. So the house seems to stand alone, like a fortress on a mountain pass, or the outpost of an unknown world. It frightened me when I first saw it, and Paul seemed frightened, too. Perhaps it's only its size that's so intimidating. It is impossible to think that Paul may own it someday. I'm sure it's not ownable. But one could love it, I think, or hate it.

Eva Weber met us at the door. She is strikingly good-looking in a Valkyrian way, and obviously a very capable and confident person. I find it absolutely incongruous that Matthew is her husband. They would seem to be precisely mismatched in almost every way. Most particularly in that her straightforward manner is such a contrast to his devout deviousness.

Eva took us to our room, our wing actually, and we didn't meet any of the others until dinner. Dinner—let's see if I can give you the picture. The room is long and narrow and dimly lit. The furniture, like the house itself, is old and massive. There are, besides Paul and me, four women and Matthew at the table. There is Eva, of course, in a rough-weave cotton suit now, very tasteful and stylish. Next to her, at the end of the table in a high-backed thronelike chair is an old woman in a long dress with a cowl collar. She has a small, delicate face and a great crown of pale hair. She seems ancient and at the same time strangely youthful. Not faded and shrunken like most very old people, but only blurred and warped like a smeared painting. It's obvious that she was once extremely beautiful. She has a stiff, rather grand way of talking, and everyone is uneasily attentive—as if to a spoiled child. She says, "My dears, how marvelous to have you with us at last," and everyone nods and smiles approvingly. She is called Margaret by everyone, not mother or grandmother, and granny would be unthinkable.

Across from me is Jonathan's mother. Rachel is soft and brown and shapeless, in a dark, heavy robelike thing, with a knob of dull brown hair at the back of her neck. There is something strangely indistinct about her, like a reflection in dark water. You can stare at her intently for a long

46

time and then look away and find the image faded. I sat across from her for two hours tonight and I have a strange feeling that if I were to meet her tomorrow on a street somewhere, I wouldn't recognize her at all. I can't see that she resembles Jon at all, but her eyes are something like Paul's, wide set and with unusually large irises. She seems nervous and ill at ease. She says very little, but seems to watch Paul almost constantly. But when he tries to talk to her, she stiffens and pulls away, almost as if she were afraid of him. I guess I'm disappointed in her. Not that she is offensive in any way, but I must have been expecting more, because she is Jonathan's mother.

The other woman at the table is called Oma, and seems to be a servant although she eats at the table with the family. She is dark and aquiline, has a rather noticeable harelip, and is so painfully self-effacing that it seems almost thoughtless to recognize her presence, and for the most part, no one does. No one speaks to her during the entire evening except to ask her to get something from the kitchen.

The conversation is mostly about the family history and the Farm, which of course, is not a farm at all. The O'Donnell family, Margaret's people, called it the Bar O Ranch, but Calvin Corey renamed it after he and Margaret were married.

Margaret has a rather eerie way of speaking about Calvin as if he were still alive, "My husband," she tells me, "is a man of great devotion and dedication. He was a minister, you know, before he came to California." Her eyes have an odd brilliance like suppressed excitement.

I ask about the house, the Farmhouse, as it is called, and I learn that the central part, the old house, was built in 1880, but that Calvin began to build onto it soon after he and Margaret were married and never really stopped until his death in '56. I want to ask why and don't have the nerve, but Eva answers. "He was a skilled carpenter and he always did all but the heaviest work himself. It was his hobby." But Margaret has another explanation. "It was a monument," she says dramatically. "The Farmhouse was his monument." Then Matthew laughs—he has a strange, snorting chuckle—and says something that sounds like, "A monumental stall—much good it did him." I may not have heard him correctly. But whatever he meant, it's obvious that Eva doesn't like it, and it doesn't seem diplomatic to ask for an explanation.

All through dinner Eva and Margaret and Matthew make a great fuss over Paul, asking him questions and catering to his finicky appetite. Predictably, he reacts by getting overexcited and bratty. I could whack him except it would be too embarrassing on our first night here. Anyway, they all seem to think he is darling, even when he refuses to eat, or answer questions, or else answers them in silly ways. After dinner he refuses to talk to anyone except Rachel and insists on sitting on her lap, exactly like a cat who must lavish affection on the one person in the room who is deathly afraid of cats. The poor woman just sits there looking acutely uncomfortable while Paul climbs all over her.

So there they are, our new family, except of course for the two Weber sons, who are away on some kind of ranch business. They grew up here on the farm with Jonathan and are just a little younger than he was—Carl is thirty-one and Miles is thirty. They must have been like three brothers. It seems so strange that he never mentioned them.

Picking up her pen, Beth added a postscript. "I slept without dreaming last night. No nightmares. I said the Farmouse was a fortress—perhaps I was right. A defense against demons."

6

‘‘H E L L O , Umm. I'm back." Paul was sitting up
in bed, tawny and touseled and sleep-warm. Beth
stuffed the letter back into the envelope and held out
her arms. "Come here, Tadpole, and give me a hug."

He padded across the floor and crawled up beside
her. "Back from where?" she asked. "Where have you
been?"

"Walking. I been walking around and watching.
And I saw a dog. Did you see the dog, Umm?"

"No. No dog. There wasn't any dog last night."

"Outside there was. There's an outside dog."

"I wouldn't be surprised. Tell me about him."

"I can't. I have to go to the bathroom." He slid off
the bed and started for the door. "You don't have to
take me. I remember where." He stopped to examine
the heavy bronze doorknob, twisting it slowly, closing
the door and reopening it, enjoying manipulating the

ornate knob and the solid weight of the old door. Out in the hall, he peered back in and closed the door very slowly, gradually cutting off Beth's view of his solemn smile. She sighed, stabbed by a sudden pang of the painful joy of Paul's existence—of Paul, who was so beautiful and vulnerable and so terrifyingly hers.

Paul dressed that morning, without his usual dreamy dawdling, and it was still quite early when they left the room. There was time for a quick tour of the rest of their quarters. The two other bedrooms were somewhat smaller than the one in which they had spent the night, but similarly furnished. If one of them had been Jonathan's boyhood room, there were no remaining traces—no boyish possessions, no faintest echo of his presence.

Paul was tugging at her, urging her on. "Let's go down those little stairs, Umm." The stairway, narrow and rather steep, led directly down to the corner of a large kitchen. Pleasantly old fashioned, the kitchen contained a white tiled sink; two stoves, an electric, more or less modern, and a charming cast-iron wood-burner; and a beautiful round oak table. At one end of the room a heavy Dutch door opened onto the patio, and at the other end a smaller door led down a short hallway to the sitting room. Smallish and oddly shaped, the sitting room, like the kitchen, seemed solid, comfortable and enduring. There was nothing, Beth thought, of Rachel here, inside these walls that had contained her for so long. Nothing soft or fluid or uncertain. These were strong rooms, thick-walled and impervious. Separate facilities or not, they were clearly a part of the whole, a part of the huge spreading structure that had been Calvin Corey's monument, or fortress.

It was time, Beth decided, to make their way back to the old house dining room, but there seemed to be no access on the ground floor. A door in the short hallway, which must have led to the connecting passage, was locked and bolted, making it necessary for them to return to the upstairs hall, and then down the long paneled corridor.

With the clear morning light radiating from the semicircular transom above the double doors, the central hall, which had seemed darkly cavernous at night, was still impressive but less intimidating. The wide staircase curved gracefully, and the fine old wood of the lofty hallway gleamed. Going slowly down the stairs, Paul put both feet on each stair, smiling his satisfaction. "No evalator," he said approvingly. An apartment child all his life, he had never learned to accept elevators with equanimity, but stairs were a special enthusiasm.

In the dining room the table was set for breakfast, but no one was in sight, so they wandered on towards the rear of the house. Beyond the curve of the stairs the central hall ended at double doors, etched glass panels set in ornate wood frames. A faint greenish glow penetrated the translucent glass, emphasizing elaborate patterns of leaves and flowers. Before Beth could reach out to stop him, Paul had turned the doorknob. The door swung open and green light flooded the hall, surrounding them.

From inside, under the great glittering central dome, the greenhouse seemed even more enormous than it had when she first saw it from the window. The air was warm and thick with moisture and rich sultry odors. His face blank with astonishment, Paul led the way between enormous plants with heavy tropical foliage, potted citrus trees, and shrubs covered with exotic flowers, fleshy and luxurious. Overhead, wide-leafed vines clung to the glass walls and sent twisting tentacles up into the curving domes.

"Is it a jungle?" Paul asked breathlessly.

"It's a greenhouse. A place where you grow things that have to have a special climate and things that don't usually grow in winter."

"What's that?" Paul pointed.

"I'm not sure. Some kind of tropical flower."

He was staring at a strange-looking blossom; a deep throat of thick blood-red petals, fringed by a border of dark feeler-like protuberances. Peering at it closely, Paul suddenly put his hands behind his back. "Don't touch it," he said.

"A good thought. In fact, you'd better not touch anything in here without asking first. Okay?"

"Okay," Paul agreed.

Farther on they walked between wide tables holding flats, in which were growing more ordinary things: tomatoes, strawberries, and various kinds of herbs. Fully recovered now from his initial wordless astonishment, Paul was jabbering happily about berries that lived in bushes instead of plastic boxes, but Beth was beginning to feel stifled, breathless, as if the thick wet air were clogging her throat. Beyond the last row of flats, steamy glass walls gleamed with morning sunshine. Hurriedly, feeling, irrationally, a little bit frantic, Beth located the outer door, and with a still busily chattering Paul in tow, burst out onto the patio.

Paul was delighted. He pranced over the flagstones, exploring the fishpond, the grotto, and the bench-circled tree, while Beth looked around curiously, orienting herself. To her left she recognized the northeast wing, hers and Paul's now, and picked out the bedroom window from which she had seen the patio and greenhouse the evening before. Only two stories high and situated lower on the hillside, the northeast wing seemed much less massive—an arm extended from a body. Another arm to the south was undoubtedly the Weber's quarters. Somewhat larger than the north wing, with wider windows, it slanted across the ridge, ending in another long veranda. Another extension, long, low, and windowless, appeared to be a storage area of some sort. And there was, she knew, yet another wing, which was not visible from where they stood; the massive stone structure that she had seen from the front drive.

It really was incredible—a great spreading octopus of a house, reaching out to surround the hillside. One almost expected to see another protuberance start to grow—a bulge of walls and windows, a swelling of siding, oozing curves of glass. . . .

"Come on, Umm. Let's go." Paul was calling to her from the edge of the patio. He was dancing with impatience as she approached. "Let's look down there at all the cages." They had reached the edge of a wide terrace, and below them the hillside sloped steeply. The slope ended in a small valley where there was, indeed, a network of fences and a scattering of small farm buildings. At the bottom of the valley, beyond the corrals, was what appeared, at first, to be an enormous trash heap—blackened timbers jutting up from weed-grown mounds of rubble. But portions of scorched and jagged walls revealed that it was actually the ruins of a very large building, a barn perhaps, destroyed by fire a long time ago.

"Where are all the animals?" Paul asked.

"I don't know." The corrals did seem to be deserted, overgrown with weeds. "Perhaps the sheep are all out in the hills in the summertime. We don't know much about sheep ranching yet, do we? We'll have to learn."

"And the bears and lions?"

"Bears and lions? There aren't any bears and lions on a ranch, Paul. You're thinking of a zoo. On a farm there are only things like cows and horses and sheep and—chickens." There was, as always, a resistance and a flinching. She wondered if there were chickens. It was quite likely, of course, that there would be. She hoped not.

"No bears," Paul said sadly. He had always been partial to the bears at Griffith Park Zoo.

The gentle touch of the early sun warmed Beth's face but, below her, the valley floor was still in deep shade. There was something unearthly about the shadowed silence of the deserted barnyard. She shivered and turned away. To the north the valley that held the barn narrowed and became heavily wooded. Tall straight evergreens and other grayish trees with twisted, almost horizontal branches clustered together in the narrow ravine. As Beth and Paul walked towards the grove, something shot out of the shadows between the trees and dashed up the slope towards them. A wave of fear ebbed quickly as it became apparent that the approaching animal was only a dog, an Irish setter. She'd never heard of a dangerous Irish setter, but she pushed Paul behind her just in case. The reddish blur came closer and became a beautiful dog, lithe and limber, fringed and feathered in gleaming coppery red. His headlong dash carried him to within a few feet of Beth's welcoming hand before he skidded to a stop and whirled away. Stopping again a little further off, he sniffed the air, his legs trembling and slender flanks heaving.

"Come on, boy," Beth coaxed. "Come see us. We won't hurt you."

The dog whimpered and danced away and then, whirling suddenly, continued on its wild dash up the hill towards the house.

"That's him," Paul said. "That's the outside dog. I told you, Umm. Remember?"

"Yes, I remember." How had Paul known there was a dog? Could he really have gotten up and gone exploring while she was asleep? No, it wasn't possible. She always heard any sound he made during the night, was aware of any movement in any way out of the ordinary. He must have dreamed about a dog and now connected it with the setter.

They walked on as far as the edge of the grove and then, turning, made their way back up the hill towards the house, slowly, because Paul was hanging back. He wanted, he said, to walk in the trees.

"Come on, honey," Beth urged. "We'll be late for breakfast. We don't want to be late for breakfast on our first day." But Paul still dragged his feet, looking

56

backward over his shoulder at the grove of trees, until, on reaching the patio, Beth found a way to divert his attention.

"Look, Paul. There's the dog again. Over by the bench. See him? He's looking at something over there near the tree."

The setter was standing, poised and alert, quivering with eager attention. As they approached, he moved sideways, avoiding them, but without taking his eyes from whatever it was that he was watching. Beth checked the tree and the bench for a bird, or perhaps a cat, but there seemed to be nothing there. Again she tried to approach the dog.

"Here, boy. Come here. Won't you let us pet you?" But again the dog danced away, circling to keep Beth from blocking his view of whatever it was that he was watching. His eyes were white-rimmed, rigidly focused, and he was trembling violently.

"Isn't that the strangest thing?" The voice was Eva's, and Beth turned to see her walking towards them across the patio. She moved vigorously, her stride long and graceful. Her energy reached out dissipating shadows. It was good to see her. Reaching Beth she held out both her hands. "Good morning, my dear. I hope you had a good night's sleep."

"Very good. Much better than usual, actually. It must be the country air."

Eva looked at the dog. "Strangest thing," she repeated. "He does that for hours at a time. He seems to be fascinated by the shadows of the leaves." She moved towards the dog. "Scat," she said. "Stop that. Scat." But the dog only circled away, still looking towards the tree.

"What's his name?" Paul asked. "Why does he look like that?"

"His name is Rufus," Eva took Paul's face in her hands and turning it towards her, kissed his cheek. "He's Margaret's dog. Your great grandmother's dog. Nobody knows why he acts that way. He's just a very strange animal." Still holding Paul's face in her hands, she said to Beth, "He's been absolutely psychopathic ever since he was just a pup. We've tried to get Margaret to get rid of him, but she won't hear of it. She's owned an Irish ever since she was a girl. Her father gave her the first one and she's had one ever since. This one must be Rufus the seventh or thereabouts. I've lost track."

Paul was squirming, trying to turn back towards the dog. "Who's he looking at? Who's Rufus looking at?" he said, twisting his head and flailing his arms in his attempt to turn around. Remembering Eva's grip on her shoulder, Beth smiled inwardly. There was a certain firmness about Eva's caresses. Paul was beginning to look like a puppet jouncing on the end of a string. Turning him loose at last, Eva took his hand. "Oma has breakfast ready. Are you ready for breakfast, Paul?"

Holding Paul's hand, Eva led the way back to the house.

"This is really fascinating," Beth said as they entered the greenhouse. "I've never seen anything like it, except perhaps the conservatory in Golden Gate Park."

"It is a bit unusual. But it's really a great convenience. It makes us almost self-sufficient here. We're able to grow a great deal of our own food, even in winter." She paused to gesture down an aisle to where fat red tomatoes hung heavily on tangled vines.

"Yes, we noticed the tomatoes. They're gorgeous," Beth said.

Just before they reached the dining room, Eva turned to Beth. "Carl came home last night," she said. "He'll be down to breakfast soon." She put her hand on Beth's arm, and Beth became aware that she was considering what she was going to say next very carefully. A scurry of fear told Beth that it would concern Jonathan, and she was not wrong. "I think it might be best if you knew ahead of time that Carl looks very much like Jonathan. The resemblance is really quite extraordinary. People used to remark about it all the time when they were children." She put her other hand on Beth's shoulder, and after a moment the strength of the grasp was transferred to the skittering panic, holding and stilling it. Beth smiled weakly.

"Thanks," she said. "Thanks for—telling me."

It seemed a foolish thing to say, but she was thankful, profoundly thankful, a few minutes later when she looked up and saw Carl standing in the doorway. She knew then that if she had not been warned she might have screamed or fainted. She had been talking to Margaret about the greenhouse, hearing how Calvin had designed it himself, planned the automatic heating and watering systems, when she looked up and Carl was there.

Silhouetted against the light, Carl was Jonathan returned from the dead. The same size and stature, the same hair, dark and heavy, the set of the shoulders, the line of brow and jaw—it was all Jonathan. Even the eyes, deep set and shadowed, seemed similar

59

until Carl came closer and she saw that they were different—terribly different.

"This is Beth, Carl, Jonathan's wife." As she spoke to her son, Eva's face looked softer, younger. Carl stood, slack-handed, looking from his mother to Beth and back again. Eva nodded sharply in Beth's direction and Carl moved quickly. He rounded the table and extended his hand.

"Hello," he said. "Jonathan's wife." His smile was tentative, lifeless, pathetically ingratiating.

"I'm—I'm Beth," Beth managed to say, "and this is Paul."

"Hello." The grin again and the extended hand, like a performing dog.

"Hello." Paul seemed wary, watchful, but there was no surprised recognition; no indication that Paul was reminded of Jon. But he'd been so young when Jon died—not quite three years old. Suddenly Paul's face crumpled in distress and Beth knew he was reflecting her pain. Pulling his hand out of Carl's, he slid out of his chair and climbed into her lap. Carl stood staring after him, grinning.

"Sit down, Carl. Your eggs are getting cold," Eva said, as if she were speaking to a child, and Carl sat, dutifully. Holding his fork clumsily in his fist, he began to eat in huge mouthfuls.

Understanding came with a pang of horror. Beth had never been good with the mentally deficient, never knew how to separate her response from her pity and revulsion. But her reaction to Carl's abnormality was compounded by his resemblance to Jonathan, and by—if there was another reason she thrust it from her, but she knew that it arose from her

60

haunting fear that there was something—different—about Paul.

At last someone spoke. "How'd you get here, Carl?" Matthew asked. "Did Miles bring you?"

"Miles?" Carl shook his head slowly. "No. Not Miles. Pete. Pete brought me."

To Beth, Eva said, "Pete is Pete Jasper, our foreman. And Miles?" she asked Carl. "When will Miles be back?"

"Miles? Be back?" Carl's face contorted with the effort to find an answer. Watching the slow lift of the dull eyes in Jonathan's face, in Jonathan's beautiful face, Beth struggled against a wave of nausea. At last Carl smiled triumphantly. "Miles went to Eureka." He nodded emphatically, sure of his answer now. "To Eureka," he repeated.

Eva shrugged angrily. "It seems we'll be doing without Miles for a while," she said to Matthew. "You'd better run over after breakfast and see what you can find out."

"Pete'll be over soon," Matthew said. "Soon as he gets through checking up on his boys. Seeing what they've been up to while he was away." Matthew chuckled.

"I'd like to know right away about the vet's report." She looked at Matthew intently.

He shrugged. "Okay," he said. "Right after breakfast."

The voices went on, Eva's and Matthew's and Margaret's, and now and then Rachel's, but Beth had begun to lose contact. She couldn't keep from looking at Carl—couldn't bear to look at him. Her mind seemed to be skidding from horror to fear, to a

61

strange undirected anger. It was sometime later that Eva's voice broke through the turmoil. She was leaning across the table, offering a platter of biscuits.

"Have a biscuit, Beth. You've hardly eaten anything."

"No thanks. I'm not used to eating much breakfast."

"Nonsense. You're much too thin." Eva's eyes, direct, concerned, met Beth's and held them. "You need building up. A little care and feeding."

Beth took the biscuit and ate it and, gradually, the turmoil faded. She found she could look at Carl without nausea.

7

"'I've sent Paul off on a walk with Rachel. I thought you might enjoy a private tour, without distractions," Eva said. Sorting through a ring of keys, she selected one and fitted it into the lock on a door that opened off the central hall, just to the right of the front doors. "I'm sorry I haven't gotten around to this before. I know you must have been curious about the rest of the house. But with Miles away I've been so busy, it was hard to find a time when we wouldn't be rushed."

"It's probably just as well," Beth said. "I've had the most incredible attack of laziness since we've been here. I knew I was tired but I guess I didn't realize just how tired. I really haven't wanted to do a thing, except sit and stare into space." It was true, at least in part. It was true that she had been strangely listless, but she had not been tranquilized beyond curiosity about the house. In the six days since her arrival at the Farm she had seen very little of it—except in her dreams. When she dreamed now of exploring strange rooms, she was aware that the rooms that stretched before her so endlessly were somewhere in the Farmhouse. And, as always, the dreams were fascinating—and troubling.

On the whole, however, the six days since their arrival had been calm and pleasant. Their lives, hers and Paul's, were already falling into a pattern. Each morning there was breakfast with all the family, in the dining room of the old house, after which everyone went his or her separate way. Margaret, accompanied by Rachel, returned to their rooms somewhere off one of the dim hallways in the upper reaches of the old house. Eva hurried off on ranch business, sometimes to her office in the library, which Beth had yet to see, or in the van to the ranch headquarters, a mile or so away to the west at a place which was always referred to as the new barnyard.

Carl also seemed to spend a great deal of time at the new barnyard. Pete was good with Carl, Eva had explained. Under Pete's supervision Carl was able to do simple chores and he loved being outdoors and with animals. Ordinarily Carl stayed at the new barnyard until almost dinner time, but one day when he had been kept home to help with some work in the storerooms, he appeared later while Paul was playing in the patio, and had spent the rest of the day following Beth and Paul around. Refusing to come closer or go away, he had stalked them at a distance, like a wild animal. He was of course harmless, but still she couldn't help being glad that Carl spent so much of his time at the new barnyard.

What Matthew did with his time was more mysterious. On the mornings when Eva worked at home he drove Carl to the new barnyard, but he returned quickly and disappeared into the south wing. What he did there for the rest of the day had not been mentioned, but it was obvious that he took little interest and played no part in the work of the ranch.

How Oma spent her time was obvious, and mysterious only in its motivation. Cooking, cleaning, washing, sewing, she seemed to work constantly and always with a kind of nervous haste. "I'm devoted to Oma," Eva said. "We all are." And Beth had thought, but hadn't said, "With good reason." It seemed to Beth that Oma did the work of at least three normal women, handling the domestic chores of the huge house almost singlehandedly. But there did seem to be a kind of bond between the two women. At the table Oma seemed to be always aware of Eva, watching her from under her heavy brows, anticipating her requests almost before they were made. Nothing less than devotion could explain such attentiveness—and such incredible industry.

And Beth and Paul had established a routine of their own. In the mornings Paul played in the patio while Beth read and watched him, from a lounge chair near the fountain or from their bedroom window. In the afternoons they usually went for a walk, exploring the neighboring hills and valleys. And each day, in the late afternoon, Eva had come to find them to ask Paul to take part in some fascinating activity. Could Paul go with her to the chicken yard to gather eggs, or to the kitchen to help Rachel bake cookies? Paul was always delighted and Beth hardly

65

less so. An hour or two of uninterrupted solitude was precious.

Beth had begun to try to write again. Nothing ambitious, short impressions, reminiscences, lengthy installment letters that might or might not be sent to Warren. The results so far had not been exciting, but it was good to be trying again. Somehow the trying seemed very important.

So the six days had slipped by easily in a calm, unaccented tranquility which, after the turmoil of the last weeks, seemed to Beth to be almost miraculous. She had not wanted to disturb the calm, to initiate anything that might bring back the doubts and fears, the tortuous indecisions, the nightly spectaculars by the midnight director. She had asked few questions and made no requests—not even to see the rest of the Farmhouse. But now she was to have that privilege.

"This is the old reception room, or parlor," Eva said. "We haven't used it for years, not since my father died. There are so many other sitting rooms that are cozier. Not as grand, but a lot more comfortable."

The room they had entered was, at first, an enormous cave of shadows. Crossing to the windows, Eva pulled back heavy drapes to reveal a scene from the past. Heavy, shoulder-high wainscoting of rich dark wood, a fireplace framed in tile and manteled in marble, an enormous sweep of Persian carpet, and a bewildering superfluity of ornate furniture—rosewood, oak and pine, velvet, horsehair, and brocade.

"It's amazing," Beth said. "Beautiful."

Eva led the way around the room, pointing out interesting pieces of furniture and portraits of ancestors—O'Donnells, mostly members of Margaret's family. In an ornate gilded frame, Margaret herself as a young girl, demurely posed in Victorian lace, her dark eyes startlingly luxurious in a small, perfect face. As they moved from picture to picture, Beth found herself missing some of the information, listening instead to the breathless stillness of the room. There was a quality of suspension—of time held back. The clocks—an elaborate glass-domed anniversary clock on the mantel, and a grandfather clock against the wall—were silent, motionless. She found herself thinking that it would do no good to wind them—they wouldn't run.

They went on then to other rooms on the ground floor, a music room with a grand piano in a bay window, a smaller sitting room, and then through the dining room to the library.

Here, surrounded by book-lined walls, was a cluttered rolltop desk and a large refectory table. The ranch office, you might call it, Eva explained. "All the books and records. Which reminds me, we still haven't gone over the books together. We'll have to do that soon—decide the best way to handle Paul's income. Perhaps when Miles comes home and I'm not so pressed for time."

"Of course. Any time." After the years of worrying about money, struggling to earn and save and stretch it, it was good to forget about it. It seemed remarkable, almost startling, to reflect that the three dollars and eighty five cents with which she had arrived was still in her purse, having neither grown nor shrunk. A relief really, at least for the time being.

They went through the south wing, the Weber

residence, quickly; a blur of large well-furnished rooms in one of which they came upon Matthew asleep in a comfortable chair, a newspaper sliding off his lap. Then there were other rooms, furnished randomly, without any apparent utility in mind. Amid pieces only old enough to be shabby, there were others that were obviously very valuable, and very old; writing desks ornately inlaid with rare wood and ivory, enormous highboys with curving fronts, thronelike chairs with great clawed feet and arm rests that ended in grotesque faces. When Beth expressed her astonishment, Eva explained, "Father was a great collector. When Lucien and I were young, the family traveled a great deal in Europe. We found that table in Austria, and the chairs came from France."

After a while the rooms began to blend together. At some point, on an upper floor, as they passed a door, Eva put her finger to her lips. "Margaret's rooms," she whispered. "We'd best wait. She'll ask you in someday."

The bedrooms in the old house were magnificent; immensely tall, narrow windows, beautiful oriental carpets, ornate furniture. Higher up on the third floor the rooms were smaller and more sparsely furnished; servants' rooms, workrooms, and a sewing room that still held a dress form, a cutting table, and an ancient treadle machine. At the end of a narrow upper hall there was a children's playroom. Unlocking the door, Eva motioned Beth inside, and waited for her in the hall.

No one had played there for a very long time. Dust eddied in small clouds around Beth's feet, and on the shelves it lay like a fine white growth on books and toys. A congregation of beautifully constructed puppets dangled against the wall, their limbs contorted by twisted strings. A bicycle leaned against a large doll house, and segments of a model train spilled out of a broken box. Everything seemed very old, strangely unfamiliar; shapes and materials that would no longer have been common during Beth's childhood. Other children must have played here before Jon, earlier generations. Something, the silence, the settling dust, the twisted puppets, was oppressive. She left suddenly. Eva was waiting in the hall.

"Did your boys play there?" Beth asked. "And Jonathan?"

"No. Never. It was Lucien's room. Lucien's and mine." Something quick and harsh in Eva's voice made Beth turn quickly, but Eva was smiling. "Well, that's about it," she said. "Unless you'd like to see the unfinished wing."

Suddenly Beth realized that she did. Realized, in fact, that her curiosity about the house had seemed from the first day to center on the closed-off section. "I'd really like to. If it's not too much trouble."

"Not at all. The entrance is just down the hall on the second floor. There was to be a connecting door on the ground floor, just beyond the dining room, but it was never cut. Perhaps you noticed the stairs that lead up to a blank wall near the end of the hallway?"

"Yes, I did wonder about that."

"The stairs were necessary because of the slope of the hill. When Father was planning Jonathan's wing he—"

"Jonathan's?"

"Why, yes. I thought you'd probably have guessed.

69

Father built for each of us. After he finished the south wing he began plans for a new section that was to have been for Jonathan. Very elaborate plans. Since Jonathan was still very young there seemed to be a great deal of time so Father planned to work very slowly and carefully, handcrafting everything. It would have been beautiful, if he had lived to finish it."

Beth hadn't guessed. The knowledge that the unfinished wing had been meant for Jonathan—had been started by Calvin as a future home for Jonathan and his family—was still numbing her mind when they arrived at a narrow door in the second-floor hallway. She had noticed it earlier, guessed it to be a closet, and wondered vaguely about the heavy latch and padlock. Now it became apparent that it had, indeed, been a closet that had been extended into a narrow passageway, ending in a short flight of makeshift stairs. Groping along the wall Eva found a switch and, ahead of them a string of bare bulbs came on, illuminating a skeletal hallway; rough floor boards and unplastered lath walls. Underfoot were bits of wood and strips of tar paper. One might have thought the construction work had halted only the day before, if it hadn't been for the deep dust and dead stagnant air, the musty ghost of old winters. The rooms they passed were doorless, unfinished, and the stairs leading down to the main floor were without a bannister. "Be very careful," Eva said. "Stay near the wall and watch your step. The stairs are slippery."

Hugging the wall, Beth suddenly found herself struggling against a surge of panic. There was no real danger, the stairs were wide, sturdy, but the unprotected edge seemed to beckon—like rushing water or the edge of a precipice. More lights came on from below, dazzling her eyes.

"You're afraid of heights?" Her hand still on the light switch, Eva was looking up from the foot of the stairs, her eyes glinting with what seemed to be amusement.

"Not really. At least, I never thought so. But that did scare me for a moment. I don't know why." At the bottom of the stairs, she steadied herself against a wall, her legs trembling.

Eva came back and stood near her, not touching her this time, but watching closely as the fear slowly subsided. "It's not surprising. It's rather a dangerous place. Construction sites always are. I probably shouldn't have risked bringing you here, but I could see that you wouldn't be satisfied until you'd seen it. So we might as well take a quick look. Then you won't have to come again."

"I don't think I'll want to."

"There's only the one room that's worth seeing, anyway. Father worked on it for a long time. It was almost finished when he died."

Like the upstairs the lower hall was unplastered, cluttered with the litter of construction, but one set of doors stood out in sharp contrast. Set in an arched frame, they were richly ornamented and beautifully finished. They opened on a very large room that seemed at first only an ocean of shadowy space in which a dangling work lamp made a small island of illumination. But as they moved farther into the room it was possible to see an enormous fireplace of gray

71

stone, darkly gleaming woodwork, and ceiling beams ending in ornately carved corbels. In the center of the beautiful parquet floor, two trestle work tables still held a collection of carpenter's tools.

It was obvious that every part of the room was carefully, skillfully made. It should have been beautiful, except—it was full of fear. She could never remember afterwards just how her eager exploration of the room had changed gradually into a frenzied search. How the threat she had felt on the stairs had returned, slowly at first, and then with gathering force, freezing her mind, taking the air from her lungs. How she came to be turning, whirling, searching the dark corners. The room was empty, silent, except the terror oozed from the walls, from the stones, clawed at the doors and windows.

A hand grasped her arm. "What is it?" Eva's voice was sharp, urgent. "What's the matter?"

"I don't know." Beth's voice was out of control, reverberating to the thunder of her heartbeat. "I just feel . . ."

Eva moved towards the door, propelling Beth before her. She didn't relax her grip until they had climbed the stairs, traversed the dim tunnel of hall, and were back in the old house.

"I shouldn't have taken you there, I suppose," Eva said. "I should have realized that it would be upsetting. Just the fact that it was to have been Jonathan's. But I could see you were determined, and I thought it might be best to get it over with."

"But what was it? Why did I feel so frightened?"

"I'm sure I couldn't say. The power of suggestion, no doubt. You were already a little shaken, and then I

72

had just told you that Father died there, in the room."

"I suppose you're right."

"Of course I am. It was quite understandable. Now you'll just have to forget all about it. And *do* get some more rest. You still look much too fragile. Let us watch Paul for you, and just take it easy for a while longer. Do some reading, perhaps. There are all those books in the library. Some of them are quite old. You might enjoy seeing what you can find of interest."

Eva's gaze was steadying, relaxing. "Yes, yes. I'd like that." It was good to be looked after, taken care of. Beth sighed, feeling the tension dissipating. She felt, suddenly, very tired.

Back in the north wing she thought it all over very carefully and decided that Eva was right. There was nothing so very mysterious about what had happened in the parlor of the boarded up wing. After hearing that it had been meant for Jonathan, and then that Calvin had actually died there, in the room. . . . it was not until then that she realized that Eva had not told her that Calvin had died in the room until *after* the strange attack of panic. Earlier she had only said that he had been working on the room at the time of his death. Beth wasn't entirely sure just when she had understood. Anyway, it didn't matter. She didn't intend to go back into the boarded-up wing, and she didn't intend to worry about it either. She smiled, thinking how much better she had been lately about worrying.

8

DEAR WARREN,

It was really great of you to answer so quickly. It feels good to know you are still there. If it weren't for your letters, I might forget that the world exists outside of Covenant Farm.

There really are times when I can hardly believe in my old existence. The city, the smog, the Yucca Court Apartments, my old desk on the sixth floor of the Farnsworth Building—it all seems like a novel about someone else—third person, if not particularly singular. Most of the time I don't miss it. There is a peacefulness here, a kind of repose that is almost lethargy. It won't last, I'm sure, but while it does I seem to be inclined to relax and enjoy it. I have thought about trying to get a job of some sort, or perhaps trying to do some writing. I think I told you that I used to think about writing. I've done very little.

To answer your question about the management of the property—there is a foreman, a man named Pete Jasper. Pete is an ominous-looking character, huge and hulking with no neck, not much forehead, and squinty eyes. He seems to have a large number of sons, I think it's about four or five actually, who unfortunately look just like him. They all live on the property at a place that is referred to as the "new barnyard." I haven't been there, but I understand that the whole sheep operation is carried out there—lambing, pens, shearing sheds, etc. There was a barn here, near the Farmhouse, but it burned down a long time ago. There are still some smaller farm buildings and corrals here, but they haven't been used in a long time. Pete seems to get his orders mainly from Eva. Miles is apparently involved, too, but he is still away, and at least in his absence, Eva seems to make all the decisions. (You'll have gotten my second letter by now, so you know about Carl.) There has been a problem lately about some diseased sheep, and Pete has been here almost every day to confer with Eva. Also, one or another of the Jaspers is always arriving here with phone messages since there are no phones here at the Farmhouse.

No, I haven't been shown any statements about the income to which Paul and I are entitled. Eva has mentioned showing me the books, but since she has been so busy with Miles away, it seemed crass to be pushy about it. They have all been so kind and welcoming. Sometimes I find our reception here unbelievable, considering the fact that Paul stands to disinherit them all. It's an awkward situation, but I did get up the courage to discuss it with Eva the other day. I said something about being amazed that Lucien had left so much to a grandchild he had never seen. And Eva said it wasn't Lucien's decision. She said Calvin left everything to Lucien and specified that the inheritance must always be in direct line through the eldest child. When I said that seemed unfair to the other members of the family, she laughed and said something about kingdoms having to be kept intact. I guess she meant that Calvin thought of the property as a kingdom. Then she assured me that Paul's inheritance would not cause a hardship for anyone. She said that by the time Paul inherits, she and Matthew and Rachel will be too old to be actively involved with the management of the property, and that their old age as well as Carl's care has already been provided for. And then she said, "And as for Miles, one doesn't need to worry about Miles' welfare, my dear. Miles will always manage to take care of himself quite adequately." I got the feeling that there are some hard feelings between mother and son, but perhaps it's only that she is angry with him right now because he's stayed away so long.

Speaking of sons, Paul seems to be thriving in his new environment. He's very much less dependent on me. Of course he can play outdoors here, and he certainly doesn't lack for attention. After having only one working mother, he is now surrounded by adoring adults. I'm afraid he's getting quite used to being the center of attention. He spends a great deal of time with Rachel and Eva, and has even been invited into Margaret's inner sanctum, which I have yet to see, by the way. Matthew has taken him fishing, and even Carl seems to adore him, following him around as if he were some kind of exotic wildlife. Which, in case you were going to ask, has worried me just a bit. But I'm sure Carl is harmless. He seems entirely placid and obedient, timid even, at least certainly in Eva's presence. And then, too, he's at the new barnyard most of the time, so he doesn't present any real problem.

And then there are the animals. You know how absolutely hypnotized Paul has always been by everything from ladybugs to elephants. Well now, after having to make do with only one rather unresponsive goldfish in the apartment, he has all kinds of pets. There is a dog, and several cats and kittens, and recently Eva had Pete bring him a baby rabbit. There are also, unfortunately, chickens. You remember my problem with chickens? I remember telling you a little about it the weekend we were in Laguna. About what happened at my uncle's farm when I was eight years old? However, the chickens are penned up quite a long way from the house and I don't suppose I'll have to associate with them. Except, Paul seems to be particularly taken with them and keeps urging me to go with him to watch them. I've only told him that I don't like chickens. Someday when he's older I'll tell him why—if I've figured it out myself by then.

I've finally seen the entire house—well, most of it. Just the day before yesterday Eva took me on a tour. It's really incredible. Eva says that Calvin, Jon's grandfather, had a kind of compulsion about building. As soon as he finished one project, he started another. The wing he was working on when he died is still unfinished and boarded up. Eva calls it Jonathan's wing.

The letter, which had been flowing smoothly, suddenly bogged down. Scribbling, scratching out, staring at the paper, and scribbling again, Beth struggled with words and phrases that had become unmanageable, unpredictable. "The interior is only roughed in except for one terrible . . ." Scratch out quickly and begin again. "There is fear . . ." She threw the page away and started over. "The weather has been very pleasant, foggy mornings and clear cool afternoons. Paul and I take lots of walks."

After the weather report, she sat a while longer with her cheek on her fist while the tension, the dim threatening echoes, died away. It was strange how quickly they went. How much easier it was here to push it back into oblivion, to drift into drowsy serenity.

Sometime later she added a brief conclusion, telling Warren that she thought of him, missed him. It was true. She did think of him, particularly in bed at night when her body reminded her that it was still young and hungry. Warren had been a good lover, skilled and thoughtful. It was too bad she . . . Well, it was too late to do anything about that. But it was not too late to make it to the mailbox before the mail truck came, if she hurried. She switched off the desk lamp. Lit by only two narrow windows, the sitting room's perpetual twilight was deepened by the dark wood of the wainscoting. But the heavy old furniture and the fireplace of rough native stone created an atmosphere of permanence and solidity, deep and everlasting as a cave. She walked slowly to the door, relishing the soft enshrouding gloom and the familiar musty closeness. These north wing rooms, which she had inhabited for so short a time, seemed to hold and encompass her in a way that no rooms had before. It was not a feeling of possession, that the rooms were hers now, as much as one of—

belonging. Of belonging, like the small drum table belonged in its place between the narrow windows.

When she had begun the letter, Paul had been in the kitchen playing with his rabbit, but now the rabbit was back in its cage and Paul was gone. Beth knelt to scratch the rabbit's head with one finger. Its utter helplessness and the soft blunt simplicity of its shape reminded her of Paul. It stared up at her with tragic eyes, as if it knew it had been born into a species destined to be preyed upon.

"Paul," she called loudly. "Where are you?"

He was not anywhere in the north wing or patio. She was on her way to the library to ask Eva if she had seen him, when she found him, in the entry hall of the old house. Arriving quietly at the top of the stairs, she saw him before he became aware of her presence. He was busily engaged in one of his imaginative games. Sitting on the hall settee, he was looking towards the parlor doors and talking to some imaginary companion. Paul's games, the conviction with which he inhabited a world beyond her reach, always fascinated and troubled her. But now, watching the play of emotions on his face—absorbed attention, confusion, and then some kind of denial with frowns and violent head shaking—she was seized by an urgent anxiety. She was about to call out to him when, suddenly, he slid down from the settee and, still facing the parlor doors, he sidled past them, his back to the wall. At the foot of the stairs he looked back and shouted, "No. I'm not. I'm not. I'm Paul," and whirling, he started to run up the stairs. He was halfway up when he saw her.

80

"Hi," he said, slowing down and smiling.

"Hello. What have you been doing?"

"I was running."

"I saw that. Why were you running?"

Noticing the letter in her hand, Paul's smile broadened. "We're going for a walk. Are we? To the mailbox?" He reached the top of the stairs and, taking her hand he started down, tugging. "Let's go." But halfway down he stopped suddenly and moved to her other side, away from the parlor doors. As they went by them he peered around her

When they were outside on the veranda, Beth asked, "Was he still there?"

"I don't know. Sometimes I can't see him."

"Who is he?"

"I don't know. Somebody."

"But you were talking to him. What did he say?"

"I don't know. I don't know his words. I'm going to run, okay?"

Without waiting for her answer, he tugged his hand free and was off, running and skipping. Beth followed slowly, thinking about Paul and his fantasies. They didn't seem to be diminishing.

The morning was heavy with drifting fog. The fog at Covenant Farm was different from any Beth had experienced before. Blindingly thick in one area, it would be no more than a wispy shadow a few yards farther on. Even on windless days it seemed always to be in subtle motion, its shifting veils pierced by a strangely distorting luminosity. Dancing through the mist only a few yards ahead of her, Paul was transformed into an infant Pan, prancing through an enchanted forest. As she watched he seemed at times to be almost airborne, as if he had become weightless, or had somehow managed a personal exemption from the law of gravity. She was about to call him back to her when she noticed a figure approaching on the path that led to the kitchen garden.

It was Rachel, small and shapeless in a gray coat that seemed much too large for her. She was carrying a basket full of vegetables, holding it before her, wrapped in her two arms. Her soft time-blurred face with its wide-set eyes and short nose was tipped down, foreshortened into an animallike mask. For a moment Beth saw her transformed—Mother Squirrel or perhaps Mother Cottontail, hurrying home to her family in the hollow log, dressed in a long gray cloak. Seeing Beth, she paused and glanced hastily around, as if considering an attempt to avoid the encounter.

"Hello," Beth said. "That's quite a harvest." Rachel only stared at her in obvious confusion. Always susceptible to contagious embarrassment, Beth cast about for a conversational gambit and, returned, despairingly, to the contents of the basket. "I love those lemon cucumbers. You know, it's really been a treat having home-grown vegetables. I've been amazed how different they taste."

Rachel's smile was limited and uncertain. "Yes. They are better, I suppose. We've always grown most of our own food."

"I've been wondering if I could help with the garden. I don't know much about it, but I should think I could learn. I've always thought that gardening would be a really satisfying kind of thing to do."

"Well, Pete and his boys usually do the planting, but we all help with the hoeing and irrigating, except Margaret, of course. I'm sure——"

"Gramma," Paul hurtled back down the path and threw himself on Rachel with such enthusiasm that she almost lost her balance. Holding him off with one hand as one might a too friendly puppy, she murmured vague protests. "No, Paul. Be careful. Don't now." As always, in Paul's presence, she seemed constrained, unnatural. And as usual, Paul seemed perversely determined to shower her with rowdy affection. Having hugged and kissed every part of his grandmother within his reach, he whirled away back down the path, shouting, "I found a whiggle, Gramma. Come see."

"A whiggle?"

"Yes. I'm afraid so. Any kind of small crawly thing. One needs a special dictionary. Unabridged Paulish."

"Yes." The nervous constraint was suddenly replaced by an earnestness that seemed out of proportion. "Words aren't important to him. He needs them less. You shouldn't worry."

"I do though. When he starts school in the fall——"

"In the fall? I don't think . . . Have you talked to the others about it? To Eva?"

"Yes. I asked Eva about the school and she said the nearest one was in Sturmville. She said she would find out about the bus."

"Oh," Rachel's eyes were again veiled and evasive. "About the bus."

"She did say that there might be a problem, since

83

kindergarten is only half day and the buses don't make a midday run. Did Jonathan and Miles go to kindergarten in Sturmville?"

"No, not to kindergarten." The dark eyes with their large irises lifted suddenly to meet Beth's. "They never went to school in Sturmville. They— didn't Eva tell you?"

"No—I don't believe she said where they went to school. I just took it for granted that it would have been in Sturmville."

"They had tutors. Carl had to have a special tutor, so he taught the other boys, too. Until they were old enough to go to boarding school. Jonathan was sent to boarding school when he was nine. Didn't he tell you about it?"

Beth realized that it was the first time she had heard Rachel say Jonathan's name. It seemed unbelievable, crazy, almost—but it was true. Why it was true, Beth had no idea. She had wanted so much to talk to Rachel about him. She had carefully gone over what she would say—deciding what could be asked and what must not be, at least for now. She had planned to ask first about his early childhood—what kind of a child had he been?—did Paul resemble him at all? And then, some time later, when she had established how much Rachel knew about the accident, she might be able to find out without really asking, if Rachel, his own mother, thought that Jonathan could ever have—done what they said he had. But not "why?" They had asked Beth "why?" But she would never do that to Rachel. She wished that Rachel understood that. If she understood that, perhaps she might not be so reluctant to talk to Beth, or even to be alone with her. But now, suddenly, Rachel stepped closer and in a voice that throbbed with some undefinable emotion she said, "Did Jonathan ever talk about—about his childhood?"

"Not very much." The dark eyes, lit now by a strange wounded intensity, searched Beth's face. Reluctantly Beth added, "Hardly at all, really."

Rachel turned away. "No," she said. "Of course, he wouldn't have. But I thought, perhaps . . ." She broke off and turned back, smiling palely, "I'd best be getting on up to the house. Margaret is alone."

Rachel hurried away into the fog and Beth stood looking after her, wondering again about Jonathan's rejection of his family. There were some strange things about them, some sad things, but no more than in many families. Nothing that would explain so complete a rejection. She'd wanted so much to ask, but it seemed out of the question with Rachel; and Eva had brought the matter up once—and then cut it off. "You really don't know anything about the family, do you? Pratt, the attorney, told us that you'd always thought that all Jonathan's people were dead. And Jonathan didn't tell you anything about his family at all?"

"Very little. I was really amazed when I found out about all of you." She had hesitated and then gone on. "And it puzzles me even more now, that I've—met everyone. I can't imagine why he didn't tell me."

"An old story, I'm afraid. Jonathan didn't get along well with his father or his grandfather. Constant arguments, that sort of thing."

"But to say they were dead . . ."

Eva shrugged. "Who can say why he did it. A reconciliation would have meant so much to Lucien before he died." There had been a sudden anger in Eva's voice and eyes, but her smile returned quickly. "But at least we can be glad that we have you and Paul with us now. Closes the breach, in a way—heals the wound." She'd patted Beth's shoulder, turned away pointedly, and the subject was closed.

Beth followed the sound of Paul's excited voice and soon caught up with him—and stopped to inspect the whiggle, a fuzzy black caterpillar. Paul was squatting, his face only inches away from the insect, which seemed to be trying to make a hasty departure.

"Don't pick him up," Paul said. "I hate it. I hate it. He said to me. So I didn't anymore."

"Don't worry. I'm not about to."

The footpath plunged down the hillside, transecting the winding road in three places before it reached the highway. The fog was thinning, and from the first crossing the gate was clearly visible far below. A pickup truck was pulled up before it. The path dipped then into a gully, and a little farther on climbed to the next crossing of the roadway. Just as they stepped out on to the road, the truck appeared, rounding the curve below them at high speed. Beth grabbed Paul, pulling him back to the shoulder, and the pickup slid to a stop. Leaning on his arm, the driver looked them over slowly and thoroughly.

"Well, well," he said at last. "The heir apparent and his mother, if I'm not mistaken."

If it were Miles Weber, and she knew it must be, he certainly didn't resemble any other member of the family, except perhaps Matthew. A sharper, thinner Matthew with a long head topped by a cap of frizzy colorless hair. Pale, sun-blotched skin stretched tight over the sharp edges of cheek and jaw, and a high domed forehead above eyes that like his father's were prominent and palely blue. But pale blue could look like skim milk—or the pale fury of burning gas.

"You must be Miles."

"Right. The smile was one-sided, ambiguous. He studied Beth and then Paul for a while longer before he said, "Not running away so soon, I hope?"

"No." Beth smiled. "We're on our way to the mailbox."

"Aha! You don't mean to tell me my thoughtful father hasn't offered to mail your letters for you?"

"Well, yes, he did, actually. But we like the walk. It gives us something to do."

"Smart move. But how about riding this once? Jump in and I'll have you down there in a minute."

Beth hesitated. "I don't know. I really need the exercise and . . ."

But Paul was tugging at her arm, his eyes shining.

"Let's ride in the truck, Umm. Can we? Can we ride in the truck, please?"

Outnumbered, Beth relented, but as she started to lift Paul into the cab he squirmed away. "No, out there. I want to ride in the back."

"No, Paul. It's too dangerous. You can't ride back there."

"Absolutely not," Miles said. "Can't say I'm delighted to be disinherited by you, young man, but I wouldn't want to solve the problem in such a messy way. Get in here." Miles was smiling, but there was an edge to his voice. Paul's eyes widened, and he climbed onto the seat without further protest.

"So, how long have you been at the Farm?" Miles

87

asked as he maneuvered the pickup in a sharp turn on the narrow road.

"Eight days. Since the eleventh."

"That long? Well, you seem to be bearing up well. How do you like it?"

"Like it? Like what, in particular?"

"The Farm. The family clan. The peace and quiet of country life. Whatever you care to comment on."

Beth laughed. "You know, I really wondered about how I'd react. I've lived in a city most of my life. But so far I've really enjoyed it. I haven't felt so relaxed in ages. I know I'll have to find something to do with myself soon. Perhaps I'll get a car and look for a job in Sturmville. But so far I've been so placid I hardly know myself. And Paul loves it here."

"Does he?" Miles glanced at Paul. There was in Miles' manner an air of constant amusement that seemed at times to border on something harsher. As his one-sided smile met the solemn wonder of Paul's eyes, Beth's arms came up instinctively in a protective gesture.

"Well, there's no doubt about its being quiet—most of the time," Miles said. "Too damn quiet to suit me, I'm afraid. I can take it for just so long and then I have to bust out. Get out among the bright lights and the flesh pots—that kind of thing. That's where I've been since I sent Carl home with Pete—out among the flesh pots. You've met my charming big brother, I take it?"

"I've met Carl," Beth said, stiffly. She was becoming more and more uncertain about how to take Miles.

He glanced at her and chuckled. "And how about

the rest of the madhouse? You on to them all by now?"

"Madhouse?"

He laughed silently, showing very white teeth. "Sure. Haven't you figured it out yet? They're all stark raving. Oh, Rachel's just mildly batty, and my dear father's perversions are fairly harmless. But the old lady's nutty as a fruitcake. And then there's Mother. Now Mother is the one to keep your eye on." Thumping Paul with his elbow, Miles said, "Don't you agree, buddy? Mothers are apt to be pretty damn dangerous. Right?"

Beth's smile was forced. She had never been good at the game of facetious outrageousness. Miles was laughing silently again.

"Well, well," he said. "So Cousin Jon ran off to the big city and picked himself out a perfect Corey wife."

Curiosity fought against a strong feeling that she'd be better off not to ask, but curiosity won. "What do you mean, a perfect Corey wife?"

The pickup skidded to a stop in the gravel near the gate. "A victim," Miles said. His smile seemed too full of teeth. "A pretty little natural-born victim."

Juggling resentment and anxiety, she returned Miles' stare with what she hoped was angry dignity, and taking Paul with her, got out of the truck. But when the letter was in the box, she turned to find Miles standing beside the cab door, holding it open. "Sorry," he said. "That definitely lacked finesse. Am I forgiven?"

The pale eyes burned in the sun-scalded face and Beth understood that Miles would not really ask for anything, much less forgiveness.

9

Twice since her arrival Beth had mentioned the possibility of a trip to Sturmville to buy supplies for her kitchen. She was anxious to plan and cook her own meals again, but there was, also, another reason. A shopping trip would absolutely necessitate some kind of clarification of the financial situation, since three eighty-five wouldn't buy many groceries. Not that she was terribly anxious about the money, but she couldn't help being curious about what Paul's share of the profits would amount to, and Warren kept scolding her for not finding out.

On the morning after her second request, Eva and Carl appeared suddenly in her kitchen, very early in the morning. Carl was carrying a large cardboard box. "Breakfast things, from the storeroom," Eva said. "Eggs and bacon and coffee. I just don't think you'd enjoy shopping in Sturmville. And with the storerooms so full, there just doesn't seem to be any point in making the long trip to Pomo. Put the box on the table, Carl."

Carl did as he was told and then stood slack-handed, grinning at Paul, who was playing with his rabbit.

"Don't know why I didn't think of it before," Eva went on. "You and Paul can have a private breakfast, get up when you want to. Sleep as late as you want. No need for you to keep farmers' hours. But don't stop joining us for dinner. Don't deprive us of your company, yours and Paul's. We all enjoy you so much."

"Well, of course if . . ." Beth was beginning when Eva interrupted.

"No, Carl," she said sharply. "Give it back." Carl was holding the rabbit.

"Carl can hold it," Paul said. "Carl can hold my rabbit."

But Carl, looking guilty and frightened, dumped the rabbit back into Paul's arms so quickly that it almost fell. Eva nodded approvingly. "He isn't good with little things," she said calmly. "He's used to large animals, pigs and sheep, and he misjudges sometimes with little things. He's really very strong." Her smile was fond, approving. "Aren't you, Carl? Very strong?"

"Strong," Carl agreed eagerly, nodding, holding out his fists tightly clenched, the blurred beauty of his face contorted into a vacuous grin. "Very strong."

Chilled by pity and something less admissable, Beth accepted Eva's food with only a weak flicker of resistance and a momentary uneasiness about the extent to which she was becoming enmeshed in an intricate tangle of indebtedness. So there had been no shopping trip to Sturmville, and dinner was still a family affair. Now that Miles was back, there would be nine at the table.

As Beth and Paul entered the dining room on the day of Miles' arrival, an argument was in progress, something about a veterinarian's report. Eva's voice was quick and sharp. On seeing Beth, she cut Miles off in midsentence.

"We can discuss it later." She stood, her manner indicating an important occasion. "I want you to meet—"

"We've met," Miles said.

Eva looked at Beth questioningly. "We were out walking. Miles gave us a lift in the pickup."

"I see. You didn't tell me, Miles."

"You didn't ask."

Oma returned from the kitchen with the main course, and the meal settled into its usual routine, but Beth could feel a difference. There was a shifting of emphasis, a heightened vibration. Its outward manifestations were slight and insignificant. Margaret was, perhaps, a little more tensely poised, and Matthew's anticipatory grin a little more constant. Rachel was, as usual, quiet and withdrawn, but what often seemed only reserve was now more obviously a full retreat. Oma and Carl alone seemed unchanged.

"So Miles picked you up on the road?" Matthew asked. "You been walking all the way to the mailbox again?"

"Yes," Beth said. "It was good of you to offer to mail my letters, but I enjoy the walk."

"Yeah," Miles said. "Only this morning it turned into a ride. We had a nice little visit. Really enjoyed it. You can imagine my surprise. I came roaring around a corner, and there they were, right in the road. Like a couple of frightened deer. Could have run them down without half trying."

Miles grinned at his father, and Matthew responded with his snorting chuckle. Eva's smile was unamused.

"But, as you can see, I didn't. Just picked them up and brought them back to the house. So here they are as good as new. But perhaps that's the wrong phrase. Instead of 'good' I should say 'beautiful.' So here they are as beautiful as ever. Yeah, that's better. Don't you agree, Ma? They're beautiful all right, and 'beautiful' means a lot more around here than 'good.' I mean, after all, they are Coreys." He turned to Beth. "Beauty is a family tradition, but I guess you've noticed that. With a few notable exceptions, like yours truly. But on the whole you have to admit that we Coreys are a beautiful bunch. Inherit it from Margaret, of course. Isn't that right, Grandma?"

Margaret was sitting stiffly upright, her hands clutching the edge of the table. The stilted formal manner had disappeared, and the long heavy-lidded eyes were wide open, intensely alive. Staring at Beth she began to speak with wild urgency. "It's true," she said. "I was very beautiful. Very beautiful. Have you seen my pictures. I must show you—"

"Margaret!" The name cut through the space between daughter and mother and ended with a snap. But heads swiveled to find Eva smiling. "You don't have any eggplant, Margaret. Matthew, help Mar-

93

garet to some of the eggplant." She turned to Beth. "The eggplant is a family specialty. Oma cooks it with eggs and cheese and spices."

"It's delicious. I thought I didn't like eggplant, but this wonderful." Beth turned to smile at Oma, but her glance was intercepted, caught and held, by the white glare of Miles' smile.

"That's right," he said. "Eggplant soufflé is a family tradition. One of many, a great many."

Eva took charge again, turning the talk to other recipes, other disguises for unpopular vegetables. Beth tried to listen, but the atmosphere quivered with tension, and from the corner of her eye, she could see that Margaret was still agitated, tremulous, her face awash with emotion.

"It was a curse," she burst out suddenly. "The curse was on me. It was all preordained—"

"Mother!" Eva had risen from her seat and was bending over Margaret. The old woman seemed to be protesting, trying to push Eva away. But then Beth was distracted by an explosion of activity from Paul. Tumbling out of his chair, he threw himself on Beth and climbed feverishly into her lap. By the time Paul was settled, curled against her chest, thumb in mouth, Eva was leading her mother from the room.

When they were gone, Rachel broke the strained silence. "It's all right," she said. "She has these spells now and then. But not often, really. Her mind is really quite—unchanged."

"An excellent choice of words," Miles said. "Unchanged is exactly right. I think you'll find," he said to Beth, "that a great many things at Covenant Farm are amazingly—unchangeable. A great many old traditions, as I mentioned before. The Coreys are great on traditions. Have you been briefed on any of it yet—family history and traditions?"

"Yes," Beth said. "A little. Eva told me about your grandfather. How he came here from New England, and that Margaret's family were very early settlers here, and owned the land."

"Not all of it. Margaret's father owned about fifteen hundred acres, most of the eastern sections, but the rest of it came to Margaret from her first husband, one Randall Bradley, a local boy. Well, the way the story goes, grandfather Calvin came to California in what you might call reduced circumstances. Down on his luck. He was from an old New England family, an educated man, and an ordained minister, believe it or not. But it seems that he left Massachusetts rather precipitously, due to some kind of scandal. Don't think he ever said just what had happened, but he definitely left under a cloud, as they say. Anyway, he came here, to the wilds of northern California, and hired himself out as a carpenter to Rafe O'Donnell, to build a house that was to be a wedding present for O'Donnell's daughter. The O'Donnell family had been here since the gold rush; and by the time Calvin arrived on the scene, they were doing very well raising cattle and lumbering. But old Rafe had another valuable asset, an extremely beautiful daughter. She had been the belle of the county since she was fifteen years old, but when Calvin arrived she had turned eighteen and had just been married off to young Randall Bradley, who had recently inherited a large parcel of land adjacent to the O'Donnell holdings, not to mention about half of

95

the town of Bradley, including the hotel, the sawmill, a couple of saloons, and a few other odds and ends. Now, considering the fact that Calvin Corey didn't have a penny to his name and had a face like the wrong end of a hard winter and was already in his mid-thirties, one might think he didn't stand a chance. But miracles do happen. Not long after Calvin's arrival, young Bradley died an untimely death. Hunting accident, so the story goes. And not too long afterwards, old Rafe discovered that the carpenter he'd hired to build his daughter's honeymoon house was spending a lot of time consoling her in her widowhood."

Eva returned then, and Miles broke off, grinning. "Don't worry, Ma. I'm not revealing any family skeletons. Just filling Beth in on a bit of the family history. Common knowedge stuff. To continue— naturally Rafe was something less than delighted, but before he had time to see that Calvin left the premises for good, what do you suppose? That's right, another goddamned miracle. And this time it was really miraculous—old Rafe got struck by lightning. Well, actually, the lightning didn't quite hit old Rafe himself, but the effect was just the same. The bolt struck the old barn—perhaps you've noticed the remains down in the valley. Rafe went into the barn trying to save a prize horse, and he never came out. Nobody knew for sure whether the smoke got him, or if the horse went crazy and trampled him, or what, because by the time they found him, the hayloft had caved in, and there wasn't a whole lot left of him. But however it happened, he was good and dead, and there wasn't anyone to stand in the way of Calvin's romance with the beautiful young widow. So the marriage took place, and they lived happily ever after, except for a brief spell of unpleasantness caused by some of the residents of the local metropolis. If you remember, young Randall had left half the town to his bride, but he had also left a whole flock of relatives who weren't too happy about all that Bradley property winding up in the hands of a sour-faced Yankee carpenter. There was talk of some kind of a showdown, legal or otherwise but—"

"Miles."

"Yeah," Miles turned towards his mother and, although they were both smiling, Beth found herself bracing as if for a head-on collision. Matthew had stopped eating, his eyes rolling between Eva and Miles with the gleeful anticipation of a front-row spectator at a Roman circus but, next to him, Oma gripped the table edge with both hands, her jaw sagging as if in panic. The collision came with silent violence, and apparently Miles gave way. "Okay," he said. "End of story. Apparently Ma thinks I'm being indiscreet."

"Not indiscreet, Miles," Eva said pleasantly. "Just misleading. As you get to know Miles better, my dear, you'll find that he has a tendency to sensationalize. The family history is quite colorful, and if you're interested I'd be glad to tell you all about it. But I'm afraid you'll find the facts somewhat less exciting than Miles' version."

"I'll try to keep that in mind the next time I get a lesson from Miles," Beth said. Everyone smiled except Matthew, who laughed so suggestively that for a moment Beth wondered what she could have said that could be taken wrong, until she remembered that Matthew laughed that way at almost everything.

10

I'm sitting in a stump in the center of a circle of redwood giants. I didn't make a mistake, I meant *in* not *on*. The center of the stump has eroded away leaving an indentation carpeted with soft aromatic redwood bark. The giant whose remains form my cradle must have died hundreds of years ago, because its offspring, who surround it in a perfect circle, are already enormous. It's a strange place, intimidating and yet comforting. There aren't many redwoods left in the area, but this small grove somehow escaped the loggers, and it has become one of my favorite places. Several times lately, I've come here to try and write. Somehow I accomplish more here than I do in the house. I don't know why exactly, but I seem to have more energy here. My parlor in the north wing should be a great place to write—it's cozy and private—but when I'm there all my efforts seem to bog down in a kind of spongy contentment. So I decided to come up here to write this, since it may not be an easy letter to write.

You asked me to "fill you in about the chicken episode" and I've decided to try. And, no, I'm not upset that you've forgotten about it. As I recall I didn't go into any detail when I told you about it, and it probably didn't impress you as being a matter of much importance. After all, who could be expected to take seriously a tragedy about chickens?

It happened when I was eight years old, at a time when we, my mother and I, were in particularly desperate financial straits. We always were, actually, but this time it was worse than usual. My father had gone to Australia and had stopped paying alimony entirely. So, in desperation—my mother was too proud to accept welfare and too, well, you might call it erratic, to hold a job—we accepted an invitation to "visit" the home of an uncle who lived in Antelope Valley. I remember being very enthusiastic about it beforehand. We were going to be living in a family with other children, and on a "ranch"—and in Antelope Valley. Such a beautiful name. I think I imagined a scene from a Disney nature film, lush and green and teeming with antelopes and other strange and wonderful beasts.

It turned out to be quite the opposite. The valley was flat and barren. My cousins —there were five of them, all older than me—resented our presence. And Wanda, who was ten and the youngest until I came, resented me most of all. And the "ranch" was a chicken ranch, a clutter of rickety buildings, terribly overcrowded with people—and chickens.

We stayed there all winter. I think it was actually only four months, but it seemed much longer. There was a peculiar endlessness about everything that winter. I remember an eternity of cold mornings waiting for the school bus with Wanda, beside a road that came dead straight from a far, flat nowhere, passed the house and went on, without a turn. The wind was always cold, and so was Wanda. The nights were endless, too, on a cot in a room I shared with Wanda and Alice—that is, they shared it with me, but it was theirs, and I had better not forget it. After the lights went out, I could hear their voices whispering for hours, and when they finally went to sleep there were other sounds; all the muffled night sounds of a crowded thin-walled house. Sometimes I could hear my mother crying.

And then there was the church, and the

endlessness of hell fire. The Hansens were
the mainstays of a little country church;
one of the kind that advertises Jesus in
neon and offers to save its converts from
a violent and murderous God. My poor
mother became an instant convert. I don't
think it was hypocritical on her part, although we were desperately in need of the
Hansens' good will. It was more that the
Hansens' God satisfied her yearning for
martyrdom. But he terrified me and, particularly in bed at night, I tormented myself with thoughts about sin and punishment. But during the day things weren't
always so bad. The school was easy for me
and I enjoyed it, and at the ranch I found
some hiding places where I could enjoy
two favorite consolations—books and
chickens.

I had learned very early the trick of
escaping into books and, at the Hansens'
I developed an enthusiasm for chickens—
at least two of them. There were other
animals on the place that I might have
preferred, cats and dogs and rabbits, but
they all belonged to somebody. The chickens didn't, at least not as pets. Nobody
cared if I played with them. I gave them
names—Robin and Higglety Pigglety—
and taught them to eat out of my hands
and let me pick them up.

I was playing with them one day out
behind a feed shed—I had made them a

little house out of an abandoned doghouse when I heard my mother calling me. I shoved a box in front of the doghouse to keep them there until I came back, and ran to the house. A man was there with my mother, an enormous ugly man with a gruff voice, a stranger really, although I had seen him, often enough at the church. The man told me he was going to marry my mother and be my new father. I was horrified. I couldn't believe that my beautiful mother could want to marry such an ugly man. But then suddenly I realized that it meant we could leave the Hansens' and I was delighted—and horrified that I could be so selfish. They took me with them then, to Lancaster to see the house we would live in after the wedding, and then out to dinner at a drive-in restaurant —a wildly exciting novelty. It was several days before I remembered the chickens, and by then they had died of hunger and thirst in the darkness of the doghouse.

I know it sounds trivial. As Mr. Freeman, a psychologist I went to while I was in college, told me, "You weren't the first kid who let a pet die through neglect, and most of them probably hated themselves for all of fifteen minutes. And you've apparently been hating yourself for eleven years." It was eleven years, then—now it's more like twenty-two. Mr. Freeman thought there was some reason, something from my earlier childhood, that made me invest the death of the chickens with an inappropriate emotional content. Which is quite likely, I suppose. But for whatever reason, those poor chickens have haunted me ever since.

Well, actually, it built up slowly over a period of time. Right after the chickens died, I felt very bad for a few days, but then there was a period during which I seemed to have gotten over it. My mother did marry Wally Trenton, and we went to live in Lancaster, and things were better for me there. At least I don't seem to have any traumatic memories of that period. I was never very close to my stepfather, but he was good for Bettina for a while, and he was kind enough to me. And I was old enough to appreciate the stability he gave to our existence. But then that marriage broke up, too, and Mother and I moved back to the city. It all happened rather quickly I think. My mother had had a second child during the marriage, a little boy who died in infancy, and after the baby's death her marriage, and a lot of other things, began to disintegrate. My memories of that period are rather fuzzy, but I guess it was a pretty traumatic scene for a while. I think Wally tried, in a clumsy bewildered way, to keep Bettina from leaving, but she was determined. So we, Bettina and I, went back to Los Angeles, and

and it was there that the nightmares really began.

The nightmares are/were (I'm not sure which tense applies—I haven't had one since we've been here, so I hope it's "were") —they *were* incredibly tormenting. There was a kind of fiendishly ingenious originality about them—midnight horror movies, produced by some evil genius for the express purpose of driving me out of my mind. They were never exactly the same twice. There might be one chicken or hundreds, dead chickens or dying ones, chickens that were half human, half alive, half burned away, half eaten by enormous worms. The only constant was that the dreams all started out innocuously, even pleasantly. I would be walking to the store, working at my desk, talking to friends, anything at all, and usually I would seem, in the dream, to be feeling particularly happy and carefree—and then suddenly there would be the chickens and the horror and I would be running and screaming—always the same words—"No, no. I'm sorry. I'm sorry. I didn't mean for you to die."

It had grown chilly in the grove, and Beth's hands were shaking. Putting down her pen, she got up and began to walk back and forth between the giant trees, flexing her fingers and trying to breathe deeply. She felt disoriented, scattered, her mind spinning out of

105

control. Suddenly she turned and ran back through the trees and out on to the open hillside. She ran until she was able to look down the hill and see the Farmhouse sprawled along the top of the saddleback ridge. She stood for a moment looking down at the great central body of the house, encrusted with gingerbread scales and a spinal ridge of turrets and chimneys, at the long neck of the south wing and the spreading arms of the other extensions. Behind her a wind had arisen among the redwoods, murmuring, whispering, but down below the Farmhouse seemed to be surrounded by windless space, enclosed in silence. She went back into the grove, picked up her pen and tablet, and started down the hill.

She had reached the patio when she saw Paul. He was standing near the wall of the south wing, facing the sycamore. There was something odd about his bearing. He stood stiffly, straight and still, his hands dangling, and as she watched he seemed to sway sharply forward, but then seeing her, he startled with surprise and dashed towards her. Part way across the yard he looked back over his shoulder and tripped and fell hard on the stones of the patio.

"Oh, Paul." He was getting up as Beth reached him. "Are you all right? Let me see your lip." There was a small cut where the sharp baby teeth had met in his lower lip, a scrape on his chin, and skinned patches on the palms of his hands, but there were no tears or screams. Paul, who usually reacted to pain with loud indignation, stood quietly, his eyes wide and dazed looking. "It's all right, honey. It won't hurt very long. Come on, let's go in and get you all patched up. You're going to have to learn not to run one way and look another." Holding his wrist she led him toward the house.

He came readily, trudging beside her, but with his head turned back. Pulling him to a stop, she moved in front of him. He was looking towards the stone bench and the sycamore, his eyes so intently focused that he seemed unaware that they had stopped, that Beth was staring at him, even of the thin dribble of blood that was making its way down his chin. Jerking him up into her arms, she hurried into the Farmhouse.

By the time Paul's wounds were cleaned and decorated with Band-Aids, he seemed quite himself again. He preened in front of the mirror, enjoying the drama of a bandaged chin and a puffy scabby lip.

"Put one here, too," he said.

"But you didn't bump your forehead. There's no hurt place there."

"There is. There!"

"That's only a mosquito bite. Mosquito bites don't need bandages."

"But it hurts." He mugged anguish, a cherubic mask of tragedy, comically expressive. "I'll die, unless."

She suppressed a laugh. "Well, all right, just this once. We'll have to make an exception for terminal mosquito bites." Paul returned to the mirror. He studied himself carefully and then sighed obviously almost overcome by the pathos of so many wounds.

"Paul, what were you looking at out there, when you fell down?" Standing behind him, Beth watched his face in the mirror. Paul's emotions were always writ large, as legible as billboard print. He stopped admiring his bandages and, as she watched, his eyes widened in alarm, rolled thoughtfully, and then narrowed. Cunning had never been a part of Paul's constitution, but there was an uncharacteristic deviousness in the way he said, "Nobody. There wasn't nobody." He turned to Beth and searched her face carefully before he added, "Was there?"

"I don't know. I'm asking you."

He looked down, hiding behind tawny lashes, then inspiration struck so obviously that there should have been a balloon over his head, framing a lighted bulb. He raised his head, smile beaming. "Let's play with my rabbit, okay? I'll go get him," and whirling he ran for the kitchen. The next time Beth tried to question him, he seemed to have forgotten the incident entirely.

11

F o r the next few days Beth made an effort to keep Paul with her. Admitting to herself that she had been enjoying, perhaps too much, the opportunity to let the others take over his supervision, to feel herself free of the constant responsibility of his care and entertainment, she resolved to spend more time with her son. On a beautiful warm Sunday in early July, she and Paul planned a long hike, complete with picnic. Carrying a bag of sandwiches and fruit, they set out in midmorning, heading towards the north with no particular destination in mind. They would hike until they were tired, eat lunch, and then come home. They had climbed to the top of the first ridge, passing through Beth's redwood grove, and were starting down the other side when they saw the three riders.

"Look, look," Paul said, wildly excited, "cowboys." The horsemen were following a path that wound its way up a steep rise, below them and to the east. As

Beth and Paul watched, the lead rider reined in his horse, pointing in their direction. The others stopped, too, and then all three galloped straight towards them, their horses scrambling on the steep hillside. Beth fought against an unreasonable desire to turn and run, but Paul was ecstatic. "Here they come. Here come the cowboys," he shouted, dancing with excitement. As the riders drew nearer, it became obvious that one of them was Miles. Paul was disappointed, Miles was Miles and therefore not a cowboy; and Beth was relieved—in some respects. To find three unknown horsemen charging up a hill straight at you was alarming, but then so was Miles.

She had wanted to like Miles, had looked forward to his return, hoping for some degree of compatibility with the only member of the family near her age except, of course, for poor Carl. But in the two weeks since his return, the little she had seen of Miles, at the evening meal, was enough to convince her that she would never have any kind of friendship with him. At the table he usually either maintained a moody silence or entertained himself by baiting people—his mother, his grandmother, Carl, or even Paul. He had not been likable, and obviously didn't care to be.

Halfway up the hill the riders' pace slowed, Miles gestured, and the other two branched off, continuing in the direction that they had been traveling. But Miles, riding an enormous red-bronze horse, came on alone. When he was almost on them, so close that Beth grabbed Paul away from the churning hooves, he pulled to a stop. Losing his footing on the steep hillside, the horse slipped, plunging sideways and leaping back up again. Miles rode the violent maneuvers easily, grinning. When the horse had finally come to a trembling, snorting standstill, Miles said, "Well well. Here the boys thought we'd flushed some trespassers, and it turns out to be the future lord and master and his mother. Where're you two off to this time?"

"We don't know exactly. Just out for a hike."

"We've got a picnic," Paul said, presumably to Miles, although his eyes were on the horse. "Want to come to our picnic?"

"Sorry. We've got some missing sheep to find. Otherwise I'd take you up on that." Miles turned to Beth. "Does Ma know about this expedition?" The horse had begun to fret, tossing his head, edging in the direction taken by the other horses. Miles jerked the reins violently, making the huge animal skitter sideways, slipping and sliding. "Surprised she let you wander around this way. Might be dangerous."

She was never sure when Miles was serious. He was grinning, his thin-lipped mouth as full of teeth as a shark's. "Dangerous?" she asked.

"Yeah, you know. Rattlesnakes. Lose your way, that sort of thing."

"We won't lose our way, but are there really rattlesnakes?"

"Not many. Look, I just thought of something you ought to see—the old town. Bradley. Part of your heritage—Paul's anyway. If you go back up the ridge to that bunch of rock and circle that next wooded knoll, you'll see a creek bed down below. Just follow the creek down to the valley and you'll come out at the ruins of Bradley. Worth seeing." He raised his hand in a gesture of dismissal. "Don't get lost."

The horse was fretting again and suddenly Miles jerked him around viciously, lashing him across the neck with the ends of the reins. The great bronze body plunged forward against the bit and then, wild-eyed, jaw gaping, came to a quivering stop.

"Good. Good. That's better. Now stand still." The words were approving, but their message, like the tight grin, was a threat of violence. Quivering, snorting, eyes rolling wildly, the horse stood still and then Miles released him, and they took off at a reckless plunging gallop after the two other riders.

Paul was disappointed. "I wanted them to come to our picnic," he said. "Does he like sandwiches? Where does he live, that horse?"

Choosing the last question, Beth answered. "They keep the horses at the new barnyard, where Pete lives, so Pete and his boys can take care of them. We'll go there some day and see the horses and the sheep—and everything. Come on. We have to go back up the hill a ways. We're going to go see an old town."

They went on for a while in silence, Paul looking back over his shoulder from time to time and sighing, obviously still engrossed in horsey thoughts. Paul's passion for horses was unauthenticated—he'd never before been close enough to one to touch it. But then passions do tend to be inexplicable. There was, for instance, the fact that, watching Miles on the horse, there had been—something. Not "something"—be honest for once—it was desire. All right, desire—but why? Miles certainly was not physically appealing, and she certainly wasn't attracted by his arrogant, almost sadistic, manner. So how to explain her hot rush of excitement? She returned to the scene—the enormous animal—plunging, sliding on the steep hillside, head tossing, eyes rolling in fear or anger—and the ease with which the man, so much smaller, controlled it—containing the fierce energy until he was ready and then—releasing it—sending it thundering across the hill. She shivered.

They rounded the wooded peak, and Beth's fantasies were interrupted by the need to choose a path down a steep incline. Below, a small creek wound its way through a narrow valley. Farther down, the valley broadened and opened into a large meadow, perhaps a mile across. The meadow was marshy, spring fed, green and lush in contrast to the summer gold of the hills. The old town of Bradley lay along the first gentle rise of the northern hills.

They came first to the ruins of what must have been a large house. A crumbling fireplace and a stone foundation around an indentation that had been a basement were all that remained. But two towering Italian cypresses still flanked the stone steps that led up to empty space, and the tangled remains of rose bushes lined the driveway. It was a beautiful site for a house, a level plateau, sheltered by the hills that rose behind it, and high enough to afford a sweeping view of the green meadow below.

A road, time-dwindled and overgrown, but still clearly discernible, ran below the ruin and on through the town. With Paul in tow, Beth explored the crumbling foundations of several large buildings, peered inside a thick-walled cement vault in the ruins of what must have been a bank, and identified a blacksmith's shop by the rusting remains of a forge.

113

Paul was very quiet. "Where did they go—the people?" he whispered, and Beth found herself whispering back. In spite of the beauty of the spot, she was beginning to find the utter isolation, where there had once been a bustling town, depressing, almost frightening.

At the end of the main street, a few buildings had apparently escaped the fire. Time and looters had taken their toll, but a few wooden walls still stood under sagging roofs. The best preserved of the survivors appeared to have been a stable. Walking down a dark alley between rows of stalls, they emerged into bright July sunshine a few feet from a human figure bending over an easel. The shock was mutual.

12

"'My word, you gave me a turn." The artist's sex was not immediately apparent, but the voice seemed to indicate that it was female. A woman of middle age dressed in baggy paint-smeared pants and shirt, her hair tucked up under a floppy high-domed hat. The face, craggy and irregular, sagged towards an over-abundance of chin. "I thought the Coreys had caught me this time for sure," she said grinning.

"Well, we're even," Beth said, peeling Paul loose from her leg. "You scared us, too. It's all right, Paul. Turn loose. It's just a lady."

The woman was working on a picture of a large, crumbling structure set back from the main road, partly hidden by the curve of the hill.

"It's the old sawmill," the woman said. "What do you think?"

The picture was solidly done, well executed, almost surrealistic in its emphasis on grotesquely deformed detail. A reality of weathered wood and rusted tin had become bleached bones hung with tattered flesh.

"It's fascinating," Beth said, "and awfully well painted, I think, but—depressing."

"Good. It's supposed to be depressing. This is a depressing place. I come here to paint a lot. It never fails to inspire me to new heights of monstrousness. How did you get here, by the way?"

"We were hiking," Beth said, "and—"

"You're trespassing, you know. Could get in a lot of trouble."

"From the Coreys, you said?"

"I'm Paul," Paul announced. "I'm Paul C—"

But Beth drowned him out. "Paul, why don't you go down there by the creek and play for awhile. Okay?"

"Can I play in the water?"

"Well, all right. If you take off your shoes." When Paul had gone, Beth repeated her question about the Coreys.

"Well, the Coreys own the land, of course, but it's that Jasper bunch you have to watch out for. Pete Jasper, the Coreys' foreman, is a real bastard, and he has a whole litter of sons who are even worse. Mean devils and the ugliest looking crowd you ever saw. They've been known to horsewhip people they caught trespassing, or throw them off the land bodily, or both. They haven't caught me yet, but I expect they will some day, if I keep on coming here."

"Why do you do it, then—keep coming?"

"Well, like I said, the place is an inspiration. Perfect example of something I've been trying to say for a long time, something about the wisdom of nature and the pitifulness of human pretensions. But I might ask you the same question. What brought you here?"

"We were just hiking. We're new in the area. I didn't realize that the Coreys were so particular about trespassers."

"Oh, they're particular, all right. The Jasper boys come through here quite often, patrolling. But there's usually two or three of them on horseback, and you can hear them coming. I try to work close to a good hiding place. I've hid out in the old stable there two or three times when they came through." The woman had moved back to her easel, and Beth followed.

"Have you known the Coreys long?" she ventured.

She laughed. "You are new around here, aren't you? No one knows the Coreys, at least no one around here. Used to be when times were better, they'd spend a lot of time traveling, living in Europe, that sort of thing, so perhaps they knew people somewhere. But recent years they've just been holed up in that dungeon of theirs, up on the ridge. Never see any of them in Sturmville anymore."

"I heard something about a kind of feud, or at least hard feelings towards them—in the town. Something about some land?"

"Oh my, yes. But that was a long time ago. That was before Sturmville was a town at all. The town was right here, then. Bradley, it was called, after one of the old families. Family named Bradley owned a lot of property around her and several of the businesses in town. It was young Randall Bradley who married Margaret O'Donnell. But poor Randall didn't have very long to enjoy his inheritance or his beautiful young wife. Died soon after they were married. Shot himself, they say, crawling through a fence. And it wasn't long at all before this Margaret O'Donnell—Bradley—married Calvin Corey, a carpenter from back east somewhere, who'd been doing some work for her father. Folks around here couldn't understand it. 'Course I wasn't here at the time, wasn't born yet, but my father was. He knew the Bradleys and the O'Donnells real well. Said he couldn't understand what came over Margaret to marry that Corey fellow. According to him, Margaret was the most beautiful thing that ever walked on two legs. Had all the young men in a hundred miles in love with her, including my father. Took him five years to get over it and settle on my mother, he always said. And here this beautiful, spoiled, frivolous girl took up with this sour-faced carpenter without a penny to his name. People in the town couldn't get over it, I guess, particularly some of the Bradley relatives who figured some of the property Margaret inherited from Randall ought, rightfully, to be theirs. That's how the feud got started."

Squinting towards the old sawmill, the woman bent over her easel. "I'd best be getting back to work now if I want to finish this masterpiece before sundown." But Beth persisted. She might never again have such an opportunity.

"But didn't Margaret's family oppose the marriage—to Corey?"

The woman straightened, waving a paintbrush for emphasis. "Well yes, of course. But there was only her father, Rafe. Her mother had been dead for years. And Rafe himself died, in another peculiar accident.

Barn on the O'Donnell place caught fire in a thunderstorm and Rafe got killed trying to save a favorite horse, a thoroughbred worth a whole lot of money. The talk started then. I mean, two accidents so close together. And Corey there, on the property, the night the barn went up. Not to mention he'd been along on the hunt when Randall died. Of course he'd had an alibi for the fire. Corey claimed he'd been with another hired hand, an old man called Frenchy, the whole time, and Frenchy backed him up. But it wasn't too long afterwards that this Frenchy disappeared. He was the drifter type. Could've just decided to move on, but people wondered. Couldn't prove anything, but there was a whole lot of talk. And then, after Margaret and Corey were married, some of the Bradleys started a lawsuit to get back some of Randall's property. The suit dragged on for years, until one real hot dry September day there was a firestorm."

"A firestorm?"

"A forest fire, in a high wind. Wiped out most of the town. Killed a few people. Randall's sister and her husband, who'd been the ones mainly involved in the lawsuit, lost a little boy. Folks said he ran back into their house looking for something. And after that his folks kind of lost heart about the suit. Just gave up, and what was left of the town moved out. Some of them rebuilt down the valley a ways, started the town of Sturmville. And little by little Corey bought up the rest of the town property, till it was all his."

Beth looked towards the east, down the strip of land that had once held stores and banks and blacksmith shops and people's houses. She could almost see the town, square wooden buildings, false-fronted—and the red devouring wind that had swept them away. There were other things she could almost see, too, things that moved in the red wind, things that had to be denied, and quickly. "But there wasn't any proof that Calvin Corey had anything to do with it at all, really. It could have all been coincidence, a thunderstorm, a forest fire."

"Sure, it could have been. Probably was. Some people thought so. And there was a spell that things healed a bit. The Coreys never were a friendly bunch, but when I was a little girl they used to come into town a bit. Even sent their kids to the public school for a while. I went to school with Lucien and Eva up till the eighth grade. After that they went away to boarding school." The paintbrush jabbed the air again. "Now there was a pair you'd never forget. You might think in a case like that, with all the hard feelings in the town towards their folks, people might have made it hard for them. You know, take it out on the kids. But nobody ever took anything out on those two. I mean nobody."

"Why not?"

"Well, it's hard to say—exactly. This may not sound sensible, but it seems to me that part of it was just that they were so goddamned beautiful. Nobody has a right to be as beautiful as those two kids were. It kind of put them—out of bounds, if you know what I mean. You didn't get close to them, not even close enough to be hateful. And then there was the way they stood by each other. Most brothers and sisters that age can't get far enough apart; but those two were always a united front, and everybody knew it. They'd come down from that crazy castle of theirs on the hill looking like a pair of dark angels, and people couldn't take their eyes off them. Lucien particularly." There was a deep sigh. The tough, humorous shield had disappeared and in its place a ghost yearned in the eyes of the middle-aged artist; the ghost of a homely girl child, born with a passion for beauty. "Lucien particularly," she said again, shaking her head slowly. "Slim-hipped, graceful, and with a face that could tear your heart out. And Eva? Eva wasn't quite as beautiful, but she was more dangerous. Kids know about things like that, and we all knew that Eva was the dangerous one."

"Dangerous?"

She came back, then, from the past and looked hard at Beth, her shrewdly comical mask retrieved and firmly back in place. "You're mighty interested in the Coreys. Thinking of writing a book or something?"

"Oh no. I'm just curious. I keep hearing things about them. But most people don't seem to be nearly so well informed." Beth amazed herself. She wasn't usually good at lies. "I just wondered how a little girl could be dangerous."

"Who knows? All I know is nobody ever crossed her. Don't know why exactly. Anyway, they went off to boarding school, and we didn't see much of them anymore for a while. Then Lucien began to spend some time in town. Not a lot of time. Didn't ever take him long to find what he was after. God knows it wouldn't have taken him long if he'd ever decided to go after me. But it wasn't just Lucien's womanizing that caused all the talk. There were rumors about a lot of other things, weird things. . . ."

Paul arrived then, dripping, from the creek, having slipped and sat in the shallow water. There would be no more talk of weird rumors, and it seemed prudent to leave before Paul decided to introduce himself again. "Good-bye, then. It's been fascinating. Glad we ran into you."

"Feeling's mutual." She extended her hand, wiping it first on the front of her shirt. "Clara. Clara Wilson."

"Beth Harper. And this is Paul." She left then hurriedly. Paul, firmly in tow, stumbled alongside whimpering.

"Picnic. Let's eat our picnic, Umm," and then, "Harper? Who's that, Umm? Who's Harper?"

In spite of Paul's protests, she didn't stop until they had left Bradley well behind. They had their picnic on the sunny hillside, and Beth played guessing games with Paul, shutting her mind to the ramblings of eccentric artists and to the mute evidence of lonely rosebushes and hearthstones abandoned to the sun and rain.

13

It had been blazing hot on the open hillside, and even in the deep shade of Beth's redwood grove it was too warm for comfort. Pieces of redwood bark stuck to her sweaty legs. Shifting her position, she brushed them off before she turned the page of her tablet. She'd finished telling Warren about the visit to the town of Bradley and the informative trespasser and even included the rumors about Calvin, emphasizing, however, their lack of foundation in any sort of factual evidence. She had scolded Warren for nagging at her about getting a full financial accounting and payment of Paul's income—she'd do it when the right time came—and had even touched on her growing uneasiness about Paul, putting it as positively as possible. So positively, in fact, that reading it over she wondered if Warren would understand that there was a problem at all. "Paul is becoming much more independent. Lately he has been playing by himself contentedly for hours at a time. Also, I've noticed that he seems to be making a clearer distinction between his fantasy world and reality. He's stopped acting as if he expected me to be able to see his imaginary companions. In fact, he's begun to be quite secretive about them." She supposed that such behavior was normal for a child Paul's age, perhaps even a little belated. But somehow she had been worried. Worried to find Paul so obviously eager to get away by himself, and so secret and devious when questioned about where he had been and what he had been doing. It would be interesting to see if Warren thought there was anything to be concerned about.

Warren's concern for her and for Paul, as expressed in his frequent letters, had been unexpected—and unexpectedly welcome. His last letter, answering the one in which she had told the story of the chickens, had been especially thoughtful and comforting. Reading it, she had suddenly wanted to—been given the courage to—write more, probe deeper. To push her way back through old shadows and, by exposing them, make them less dark and threatening. She had come to the grove today resolved to do just that. To conjure up more memories and capture them with words—words that she might or might not include in her next letter to Warren.

Taking a fresh sheet, she began at the top.

My mother called herself Bettina. It wasn't really her name, but it was like her—beautiful and unreal. She was small and slender, vulnerable, pathetic, and without mercy. She needed other people desperately, and drove them away from her. But I stayed because I was only a child and spellbound. For a long time I saw only with her eyes, played her games, and never dreamed that I could live outside the world of her enchantment.

My father, my real father, had gone away when I was only a few years old. I don't know why. Perhaps he finally saw through the gingham and lace, the fragile, willowy charm, and glimpsed the grasping, vengeful thing beneath. But for whatever reason, he disappeared and left Bettina and me alone together. We were alone together a lot in the next few years, even though we moved in and out of apartments, and other people's lives, looking I guess for some kind of permanence and support. But nothing lasted, and we were often alone. During those times we lived, I think, on dreams. Dreams and stories and legends. Bettina recited nursery rhymes, and long stories about her childhood, fairly tales, and pathetic personal tragedies and wonderful romantic legends about the man who had married her, fathered me and then walked out of her life.

I loved the stories, lived in them. I knew her childhood friends better than I knew my own, cried over her tragedies, and believed implicitly in the beautiful prince charming who had been my father. The

125

legends never explained why he had gone away, but one of Freeman's theories was that I had made up my mind very early about who was to blame. I'm not sure he was right. I'm not sure I blamed myself for my parents' divorce. And I don't think Bettina meant for me to, at least not consciously. But to blame herself would have been to destroy the legend.

My father—I couldn't really remember him, but there were pictures—tall and blond with almost too-regular features. Beautiful, Bettina would say, like a Greek god. They met at a dance. She would take my hands and twirl me around the floor until we were both dizzy. Some enchanted evening, you will meet your true love, she would sing. When we stopped I would say, "Tell about skiing. Tell about how he won the race." I asked for all the stories again and again because it was when the stories were over that Bettina's eyes might become wild and wet, her fingers would tangle, and she would push me away. Sometimes she locked herself in her room for hours at a time, and when I knocked on the door she told me to go away.

Later, after her divorce from Wally Trenton, Bettina began to take pills. She kept taking more and more until not only the wild spells went away, but the games and laughter, too. She became not Bettina but a pale, dull shadow, and gradually the enchantment faded, even for me. Not long after I graduated from high school she took too many pills one night and didn't wake up. She may not have meant to.

Beth took a long, deep breath. The air seemed thick with heat, stifling. She could feel sweat running down the backs of her legs. Pulling out the front of her loose cotton blouse, she blew downwards, welcoming the cooling tingle of evaporation on neck and breasts. It was just too hot to write—too uncomfortable. She hadn't accomplished much, but it couldn't be helped. How could one concentrate on exploring the past when the present insisted on pressing down on one like a great, feverish incubating hen? Now there was a significant simile! Might be worth thinking about—if only it weren't so damn hot. She found herself thinking longingly of her cool, dim parlor.

It was much cooler in the house, particularly on the ground floor. She took a bath and pulled on a loose caftan. Taking a book, she went down to the parlor. She had been there only a few minutes when Eva came in with Paul.

Eva was on her way to the new barnyard, and she was thinking of taking Paul along if Beth didn't object. Paul could look at the animals while she went over some business matters with Pete. There was no need to ask Paul if he wanted to go. "The horses live there," he reminded Beth, his eyes glowing. When they had gone, Beth returned to her book.

She was rereading *A Connecticut Yankee in King Arthur's Court*. It was from a beautifully bound set of Mark Twain's works that she had discovered in the library. She was making her way through the entire set, rereading old favorites, as well as exploring some she had missed.

Stretched out on the couch, she tried to reenter Twain's Camelot, but without success. Her mind seemed stuck on a kind of sensory autopilot. She was aware of deep enveloping silence, of the hot glare beyond the narrow windows and the dim seclusion of the room. The oppressive weight of the heat was shut away outside the walls. Around her the air, enclosed and shadowed, was neither hot nor cold. Beneath the loose caftan, her body, naked, felt skinless, blended with air, afloat in a soft sea of blood-warm fluid. The floating sensation deepened, and she slept, briefly.

A sound wakened her. She opened her eyes slowly in the dim light and saw without surprise that it was Miles. He closed the door behind him, locked it, and came to stand beside the couch, looking down at her. Book still clasped to her chest with both hands, she lay without moving, looking up at the sharp hatchet face, the pale eyes, feeling first, briefly, revulsion and denial. But the face came closer, blazed with cold punishing demand, threatened, paralyzed—and released some dark mindless thing that surrendered eagerly, inviting the grasp and shove, the hard hands jerking away the caftan, the brief brutal demands, and submitted eagerly, whimpering, to the violent battering scourging force.

When he had gone, she took possession of herself slowly, as if returning from a vivid and violent dream. Alone again in the dim room, it seemed almost to have been a dream, a nightmare, a mad sexual fantasy—except that she was naked, sprawled, bruised, and throbbing. A swift needle of alarm penetrated the haze. Someone might come in—Paul, Paul would be returning soon. She pushed herself upright. Clumsily, limp-limbed, she struggled into the caftan and ran from the room.

Driven by frantic, guilty haste, she was bathed and dressed before full realization came, and with it a raging confusion of anger and disgust. Pacing, grimacing, gesturing, she alternately raged at herself and made frantic attempts to throw up smokescreens of rationalization.

He was everything she most disliked in a man: sarcastic, sadistic, arrogantly macho. He had called her a victim, and she had proved him right. An all too willing victim. How he must be gloating now, remembering. Remembering, she shuddered so violently that her ears rang. She groaned, caught in a crushing confusion of disgust and remembered passion. Her response had been violent, shattering, final—unlike anything—any time—except occasionally with Jonathan. It was unexplainable, unexcusable. She had excused her lack of response to Warren by blaming his lack of commitment, his too-skillful lovemaking. And yet she had responded violently—to rape. She had validated the obscene fantasy of the rapist, that his victim enjoys the attack.

And yet it had not been rape. There had been no threats, no struggle, no screams for help. She seized on the thought eagerly. Perhaps she had chosen—or at least her body had chosen—to accept Miles, to use him. She was, after all, a normal woman at her sexual peak, and she had been without a man for a long time. Perhaps she had used him as much as he her.

She should accept the fact calmly and without prejudice, and yet—she knew it was not the truth. She knew, obscurely and yet with absolute certainty, that something had prevented her from choosing freely.

That night at dinner Miles' manner was entirely unchanged. As usual he said very little to Beth. He issued curt orders to Oma and then ate silently during most of the meal, emerging from his self-imposed isolation to torment Eva through Carl.

"Carl. How'd it go today? Get those pigs all tagged?"

Carl looked up, startled, unaccustomed to being included in the conversation. "Yeah," he said eagerly. "I helped. I helped Pete with the pigs."

"What did you do, Carl? You write down all those tag numbers so we can keep track of them? You put those numbers in the book?"

"No," Carl said. "I held them. I held the pigs for Pete."

"How come you didn't write down those numbers, Carl?"

Carl looked at Miles pleadingly, knowing he was being teased. "You know, Miles. You know I can't."

Beth found she was having trouble swallowing. Her tricky stomach, which in the past had sometimes reacted to emotional upheavals by upheavals of its own, seemed on the point of reverting to its old habits. Hurrying Paul through his meal, she excused herself and was leaving the table when Eva asked if she were feeling well.

"You don't seem quite yourself," she said. "And you hardly touched your dinner."

130

"I'm fine," Beth said. "I think it's just the heat." She didn't have to look at Miles to see the grin. She could still see it, chalk white and triumphant, as she hurried down the hall.

14

T H E heat wave lingered. The days were brilliant, the dry air spicy with the smell of sun-baked vegetation, the nights breathless and strangely hushed, as if even the frogs and crickets had been silenced.

"It will break soon," Eva said. "It never stays hot for long. The fog will roll in and cool things off, and then, in a month or so, the rains will begin. I always feel relieved when the rain starts because of the danger of fire, you know. At this time of year it takes only a spark and a high wind and—holocaust. There's always a kind of tension this time of year." She looked at Beth intently. "You'll feel better when the rains come, more relaxed."

Eva had been right about the tension, but Beth doubted it could be attributed to the weather. The opposing forces, she was sure, were much more internal than wind patterns and high-pressure systems, if just as mysteriously uncontrollable. The thing with

Miles had, it seemed, precipitated a frenzy of introspection, inward exploration—and agony. The agony was not, she decided, due to any lingering aftereffects of outdated moral preachings. She had long ago accepted her body as hers alone to do with as she saw fit as long as no one else was wounded. Nor was the agony, at least not entirely, due to her chagrin at finding that she had verified Miles' assessment of her as willing victim and given aid and comfort to his egomania. It was more that she was completely unable to explain what had happened in terms of her own self-image, her own likes and dislikes, needs and desires. She had begun to be tormented by a persistent feeling that something was hidden from her, something terribly basic and vital.

But if she were unable to discover any explanations, she did at least come to a firm decision. It would not happen again. Now that she was forewarned, prepared, not only for what Miles might do, but for her own reactions, there would be no repeat performance of the violent and degrading coupling on the couch in the parlor. There would be no immediate opportunity to test her resolve, since Miles had gone away again on ranch business, but she didn't need to test it to be certain. It would not happen again.

Along with the weather, Beth's pattern of living at Covenant Farm had begun to change. The lethargy that she had experienced during her first weeks at the Farm had not been entirely dispelled, but it was intermittent now, interspersed by periods of almost compulsive activity, cleaning, gardening, and prolific if garbled scribbling. The nights, too, had changed. They were still free from nightmares, but they had

133

become, at times, almost free from sleep itself. Lying awake hour after hour in the muted darkness, her mind raced, reaching ahead or pushing its way back, further and further, down dim corridors.

It was because of the insomnia, perhaps, that the writing began to grow and change. Just as she had discovered long before that writing could sometimes banish the mad producer of midnight horror movies, she now found that it could also mollify or exhaust this new demon who was keeping her eyes from closing. Turning on the light in the depth of the night, she would pick up her pen and write feverishly, precipitately, almost unconsciously, until her fingers became limp and heavy, and then her eyelids, and at last she slept.

Read the next day, the results of these midnight attacks of verbalism were disappointing, undisciplined, fragmentary, without any value beyond their original effectiveness as a sedative.

"Rock-a-bye baby in the tree top." Wanda had an absolutely gorgeous doll with long fat curls but I wasn't allowed to touch it except sometimes when we played a certain game. Sometimes when we were alone she would take off all the doll's clothes and make it roll around on the bed with her Raggedy Andy doll or with my old teddy bear. She said the doll was doing things bad girls did with boys. Sometimes she let me make the doll roll around on the bed, and when it was my turn, I felt warm and shaky. When the

134

game was over, Wanda would beat the doll with a belt and make her kneel down to say her prayers so she wouldn't go to hell. When the doll knelt, her legs bent straight backwards at the hips because she didn't have any knees. Wanda made the doll cry and sob and beg for forgiveness, and then she said that God had forgiven her. I prayed too, but I couldn't bend the way the doll did and I could never be sure that I was forgiven.

My baby brother was better than a doll. His name was Andrew Trenton, but we called him Andy. After he was born, Bettina was sick for a long time so I took care of him a lot. I took him for walks in his stroller and fed him his bottle and sang to him Rock-a-bye baby. He held on to my finger with his round pink fingers. He was a lot better than Wanda's doll, but when I was nine years old I went away to camp, and while I was gone Andy died of pneumonia. I can't even remember if I cried.

And on another night she scribbled:

Why did you pick me Jon that night at Elspeth's? Katy was there and that sexy Greek girl and you picked me. Why did you pick me Jon?—Lying loosely together resting exhausted coming back slowly from the beautiful annihilation of Jon's love— Beats me All I can remember is that god-awful dress—I know You said you didn't like it I threw it away What was wrong with it?—I don't know Didn't go with those wonderful crazy eyes—Crazy?—I ask quickly thinking don't Jon don't tease that way—Yeah—Taking my chin between his thumb and finger his smile like a lovebite—Crazy doomed innocence Like a kitten on the freeway Guess I thought it might as well be me—He laughed but I went on asking my dumb questions until his smile turned into bare teeth and then into something frightening—Okay Bethy have it your way We needed each other You might even say we deserved each other—His hand over my mouth—It might be smart to leave it at that Okay Bethy?— Okay Jon—"

The heat lasted for five days and then the fog came back, flooding in over the western hills and falling into the valley in great curling waves, like the slow rolling breakers of some ghostly ocean. And as Eva had said it would, the tension lessened; but whether from the change in the weather or because of Miles' absence, Beth wasn't certain. Miles had gone to supervise some work at the summer pastures, and there was less tension at Covenant Farm, particularly in the evening in the dining room. For the last few nights Matthew, too, had been absent from the evening meal.

"Did Matthew go with Miles to the summer pastures?" Beth asked Rachel. Eva was engaged in a conversation with Margaret at the time, but she turned to listen to Rachel's answer.

"No. No, I don't think so," Rachel said, glancing at Eva nervously. "I think he just isn't feeling very well."

Eva smiled grimly. "Now Rachel," she said. "Beth is a part of the family now, and as such she's entitled to the truth about the family, even when it's painful. My dear husband, Beth, is a periodic drunk. Well, actually he drinks fairly steadily, but most of the time he's able to keep it more or less under control. But now and then he goes on a real spree. Sits down in a comfortable chair and drinks himself into total oblivion. Afterwards he's usually good and sick, and then, for a few days, fairly sober. Then it all begins all over again."

"I didn't know. I mean, I did know that he drank some, but I didn't—"

"It's all right. We're all quite resigned to it by now. It must have been the change in the weather this time. A sudden change in the weather often seems to bring on one of his attacks. He still suffers periodic pain in his leg and back, and the dampness seems to aggravate it. The pain becomes an excuse for the drinking."

"He brought it on himself." Margaret's voice was high-pitched, charged with dramatic intensity, just as it had been when she had reacted so strangely to Miles' mention of her beauty. "He had been warned. He should have known better. He should have known that—"

"Margaret! Remember your promise." Eva spoke calmly, but each word was weighted, compelling as a

137

scream. "You promised not to upset us all at dinner-time again."

The luxurious oval eyes set in the warped face stared wildly, stilled under Eva's gaze, and fell. "Yes," she mumbled. "Yes, you're quite right, Eva. I—I'm sorry."

After a moment Eva turned to Beth. "Margaret was referring to Matthew's injury," she said. "He was injured in a collision with a logging truck. Father had warned him about the brakes in an old car that had been sitting around the place for years, but one day, when nothing else was available, Matthew decided to go into town, in a hurry. There was a logging truck, on a sharp curve, and. . . ." She shrugged.

"I'm going to town," Paul announced. "I'm going to ride to town on Miles' horse."

"That might be a rather dangerous way to start out," Eva said. "One has to start out slowly with horses, young man. Perhaps with a pony first. You have a lot to learn before you try to ride a horse like that red monster."

"Yeesss!" The prolonged affirmation issued slowly through a spreading smile. "Yes, a pony." For a moment Paul seemed stunned by joy, and then, coming to life, he slid down from his chair and ran to Eva. "Really, a pony? Really, Eva?"

"Well, I don't see why not, if your mother agrees. But you'll have to learn about ponies first. How to feed them and take care of them."

"I'll learn. I'll learn all about ponies." Paul ran to Beth. "I'm going to learn about ponies, Umm. Okay?" Carl's chair was next and Paul tugged at his arm. "I'm going to get a pony, Carl."

Carl nodded violently, blinking and smiling. "That's good, Paul. That's good. I'll help you. I'll help you ride the pony." For a moment he bounced in his chair like a five-year-old until, catching Eva's gaze, he suddenly quieted and removing Paul's hand from his arm, he bent his head over his plate. Watching, Beth steeled herself for the hundredth time against the pain of the similarities between Carl and Jonathan—and the differences.

Climbing back onto his chair Paul said, "I'm going to school to learn about ponies."

Everyone laughed. "Speaking of school," Beth said. "Have you found out anything about the buses, and when school starts this year? It shouldn't be long now."

"Yes, I have, as a matter of fact, and I'm afraid the news isn't good," Eva said. "There is no midday bus, so Paul would be stranded for half a day with nothing to do. We'll talk about it some more, but it begins to look as if—"

"Yes," Beth said. "Well, perhaps it's all for the best. I know some teachers seem to feel that it would be good for most children to start later, particularly boys."

She was almost relieved to know that the decision had been taken out of her hands. School now might be good for Paul, but then again, perhaps it would be too much to ask of him. He seemed at times to be becoming more independent, and at others to be regressing, sinking deeper into his fantasies. If he went to school now, he might be teased, ridiculed by the other children. And then, too, if people in Sturmville still harbored hard feelings against the Coreys, it was possible that starting school might be made especially difficult for Paul. It might be best to wait until he was older, tougher, to keep him with her another year. She could teach him herself. There was a great deal that he could learn here—

"There's so much to be learned on a farm," Eva said. "So much Paul can learn here."

"Yes," Beth agreed. Yes, Eva was right. Certainly, Eva was right.

15

REACHING the end of a row of cabbages, Beth straightened, looked at her watch, and realized that Paul had been gone for a long time. He had picked some summer squash under her supervision and had wanted to take them to Oma in the kitchen. A special kind of wordless rapport had developed between Paul and the dark, silent woman, and he had begun to spend quite a bit of time "helping Oma." But this time Beth had asked him to come right back and he had agreed, nodding solemnly; but now almost an hour had gone by and he hadn't returned. Frowning, Beth put the hoe in the garden shed and hurried towards the house. She hoped he really was with Oma. He had been disappearing so often lately, sneaking off by himself. It was unlike him; and his reluctance, on returning, to talk about where he had been and what he had been doing was even more uncharacteristic. It worried her.

As she climbed the steep path that led from the garden to the house, she heard the sound of a car motor and, looking down the hill, saw the van winding its way towards the highway. That would be Eva on her way to bring Carl home from the new barnyard. With Miles away and Matthew incapacitated, she had been delivering Carl to the new barnyard almost every day, and several times lately Paul had gone with her. It was possible that Paul was with her now, although usually Beth was consulted, or at least informed.

The garden path climbed towards the front of the house, and then merged with the circular driveway. Even now, hurrying, anxious, she found herself pausing for a moment to look up at the stone-faced walls and the dark empty windows of Jonathan's wing. It was the weirdest thing how everytime she saw it it was the same—the sudden jolt of surprise and consternation, and something like recognition. As if some morbid inner voice were saying darkly, "Oh, oh. I was afraid of this." Smiling grimly at her own foolishness, she hurried past the stone walls.

The nearest entrance was by way of the central portico and the huge front doors of the old house. As she closed the heavy doors behind her, she became aware that she was not alone and, looking up, saw Margaret, halfway down the curving staircase. Clutching the bannister with both hands, the old woman seemed to be wavering as if about to fall. Beth raced up the stairs. "Here, let me help you. Are you all right?"

"No, I'm not all right." The tone was petulant, sulky. "I'm tired of being all alone. Rachel went down to help Oma with the bread, but she promised to hurry, and it's been hours. So I just decided I'd go down and find her."

"Well, why don't you let me go find her for you? Here, let me help you back up to your room, and then I'll run down to the kitchen and tell Rachel you need her."

"Well," Margaret hesitated, obviously somewhat reluctant to give up her daring plan to appear suddenly in the kitchen and confront Rachel with her neglect of duty. "Well, all right." She turned unsteadily, and with Beth's support began to make her way back up the stairs. When they reached the door of her room, she did not relinquish her grip on Beth's arm. "Just help me to my chair before you go. I'm feeling rather shaky," she said. It was the first time Beth had been inside the suite of rooms inhabited by Margaret and Rachel.

The room they were entering was dimly lit and so crowded with shadowy shapes that for a moment it seemed to be as densely and weirdly inhabited as a Hieronymus Bosch painting. But as Beth's eyes adjusted to the dim light, she could see that the strange shapes were only a crowded confusion of articles of furniture; high-backed chairs, fringed lamps, coat trees hung with pieces of clothing, tables, what-nots, a canopied bed, and two huge pedestal-based statues. Heavy drapes were pulled across all but one of the long, narrow windows, and the air was dry and warm and smelled of rose petals and dusty years. With Margaret directing, "This way—be careful of that lamp—no, no—over there—by the window," they made their way across the room to where a large, comfortable quilt-draped chair was drawn up before the one uncovered window. Margaret sank into the chair sighing. Beth was arranging the quilt over her legs when suddenly she pushed Beth aside and leaned forward to peer out of the window.

The greenhouse was directly below and beyond it the patio, cool and dim in the gray fog, the sycamore as static as a painting in the windless air. For what seemed to be several minutes Margaret stared out the window, but when Beth moved as if to go, she lifted her hand in a restraining gesture. "Calvin loved the patio," she said. "He used to sit there, on the bench by the hour. I would look down from this window and see him there, hour after hour." She went on staring for some time before she sank back, sighing again, and reached shakily for a glass on the table beside her chair. It was almost empty.

"Could I get you some more water?" Beth asked.

"Yes, yes," Margaret waved her hand wearily towards a door. "The bathroom's in there." The hand drifted down to hang limply over the chair arm, and the delicate head under its heavy load of pale hair sank forward. In the bathroom Beth filled the glass at a marble basin and was picking her way back through the maze of furniture, when she noticed the picture above the mantel.

It was a portrait of a man in late middle age, a narrow, angular face, the eyes pale-rimmed and deep-set. Something stirred in Beth's memory. There was indeed a resemblance to the picture that Jon had thrown away because it reminded him of his grandfather. But in this face there was something more, something that reached out and touched deep, quickening the heart and changing the rhythm of the breath. For an uncanny moment Beth felt stilled, drained, possessed by a resignation as cold and final as that of a bird before a weaving snake.

"Yes, that's Calvin." Margaret's voice was high and tremulous, totally unlike the sulky mumble of a few moments before. Beth turned to find a transformation. Sitting tautly poised on the edge of the chair, Margaret was staring at the portrait with dilated eyes. "Do you know what he did for my love?" she said. "Have I told you? Do you understand what was sacrificed?" The erectly held head erased the warp of cheek and jowl, and the sagging eyes had widened into perfectly shaped ovals exquisitely slanted over high cheekbones. In the dim light of the cluttered room it was almost as if time had rolled backwards and the old woman had been replaced by the girl whose beauty had been a local legend.

"No," Beth said, uncertainly. "I don't think—"

"Come here," Margaret said. "I must tell you what was done for my accursed beauty." A thin hand clawed, clutching Beth's wrist and slopping water from the glass. "I was already married, you know, and even if I hadn't been, my father would never have permitted. . . . So Calvin bargained for me—for the power to overcome the obstacles. He made a convenant with—the powers of darkness. He—sacrificed—his—soul."

The last words were pronounced slowly and with great emphasis. Staring into the mad eyes, Beth felt something inward contract painfully with pity and fear. She struggled weakly to free her arm, but Margaret's grip was amazingly strong.

145

"You don't believe me," Margaret said. "You don't believe such things are possible?"

"I don't know," Beth said. In the face of such conviction, argument seemed of little use.

"Oh, but it's true. Terribly true. There are people who have access to extraordinary powers. Calvin was born into such a family. He had a great-grandmother who used her strength only to summon the power to heal and prophesy, and she was hung as a witch. My husband used his to summon the forces that would help him gain his heart's desire." The old woman was staring at the picture, her face glowing with a wild elation. But as Beth watched, the pride faded and died away and was replaced by a mask of grief. "But someday, he will have to pay the price."

"Someday?" Beth asked.

"Someday," Margaret repeated. "When the covenant is broken. When there is no one, no Corey heir, to maintain the pact. But that will be a long time now, a very long time, now that we have Paul."

At that moment there was a scuffle of movement somewhere in the room behind them and then a heart-stopping moan, low and quavering. Beth whirled, wrenching her arm free from Margaret's grasp. The Irish setter was standing near the bed, his muzzle lifted. At Beth's gasp, he stopped howling and stood staring at her, trembling, his sad doggy eyes fixed pleadingly on her face. There was, just as Eva had said, something strange about him. Something pathetic. A bewildered, demented quality, like a laboratory rat that has been exposed to unpredictable, contradictory stimuli. After a moment he turned away, and slinking through the jungle of furniture, he made his way to the door. When Beth turned back to Margaret, the old woman was huddled in her chair, her face collapsed into a wrinkled caricature of querulous old age.

"Poor neglected thing," she said. "He needs to go outside. Rachel should have put him out hours ago."

"I'll let him out on my way to the kitchen," Beth said. "And I'll tell Rachel you're waiting for her." Her only thought was to get out of the dim, crowded room, and away from the crazy old woman. Once outside the door, she began to run, the setter following close behind. In the entry she stopped only long enough to release the dog, and then ran on towards the kitchen.

Warm and bright and filled with the wonderful aroma of baking bread, the kitchen seemed a haven of normalcy. Oma was working at the sink and bent over the table, Rachel was kneading a large mass of dough. They looked up, startled by Beth's precipitous entrance. Before she could catch her breath to speak, Rachel was at the sink, hastily washing her hands.

"It's Margaret," Beth gasped. "She wants to see you. She seems—rather upset."

Rachel paused long enough to search Beth's face with her strange animallike eyes, and then hurried from the room. As Beth turned to follow her, she became aware of voices in the central hallway. It was Eva and Carl, returned from the new barnyard, and Paul was, indeed, with them.

Paul was dirty and touseled and in exceedingly high spirits. Back in the north wing, Beth followed him around with a wet wash cloth as he danced

147

around the room singing, "I'm going to get a pony, a pony, a pony." Pouncing, Beth pinned him against the wall and applied the cloth to his grimy face.

"Who says you're going to get a pony?"

Paul tugged the cloth away, exposing a damply radiant countenance. "Eva said. Eva said," he crowed.

"Oh, she did, did she? Did she say when, by any chance?"

One hand enveloped in the wash cloth, Paul pranced around Beth in a circle, so that she had to turn with him. Pausing in mid-step, he considered the question. "Not today," he said thoughtfully; and then, triumphantly, "After a while. Eva said, after a little while." Prancing again, he sang, "After a little, little, little while."

Beth sighed. Paul with a pony was a complication she didn't need just at the present. "Stand still just a minute, can't you? You're going to make us late for dinner."

She entered the dining room that night with some trepidation, but Margaret was her usual self, stiffly formal and aloof. If she remembered anything at all about the encounter with Beth and the weird things she had said, she gave no outward sign. The conversation was mostly about a summer that the entire family had spent in Switzerland when the boys were young children, and Margaret's contributions to the reminiscences were rational and coherent. It seemed evident that her attacks of madness were temporary.

148

16

I T wasn't until Paul was safely in bed and asleep that there was time to think about the significance of Margaret's ravings. It seemed to be a classic case of delusions of grandeur. What could be more tragically romantic, more ego flattering, than to believe that you had been worth the ultimate sacrifice? Other men had sacrificed fortunes, thrones, even their lives for the women they loved, but how many women had inspired such passion that its satisfaction outweighed the value of a man's soul? It really was the ultimate in self-aggrandizing fantasies. And a fairly gruesome one, if Margaret really meant that the powers summoned by Calvin removed the obstacles by doing away with her father and first husband.

Remembering what Matthew had said about Calvin's passion for the land, it occurred to Beth to wonder if Margaret's fair self had been his only interest, or if his everlasting soul had been bartered for both the daughter and the ducats, as it were. And what was it she had said about Paul—just before the dog started howling? Something about a Corey heir, and the covenant. But it was useless to worry about the wanderings of senility. Margaret was a very old woman and as such she was entitled to arrange her delusions to suit her preferences, as far as Beth was concerned. Except she did wish she'd leave Paul out of them. And she herself would just as soon not be exposed to them again, at least not alone with Margaret in that creepy, cluttered room.

The scene returned, too vividly. Deciding it would be best to turn her mind to other things, Beth settled down in the rocking chair with a book. After a few minutes she decided to try writing but that too failed to hold her attention. She tried meditating but her mind, never too obedient about staying receptively blank, refused to cooperate. Moving restlessly around the room, she stopped now and then to stare out the window. It was a bright night, the moon almost full with only a few clouds scattered in a windy sky. Opening the window she leaned out into the cool restless air. Below her was the greenhouse and a sea of pale, empty eyes—dull moons trapped in glassy planes backed by lush green darkness. A garden of darkness where strange things bloomed—fleshy flowers, blood-red berries, pretty girls all in a row. Closing the window quickly she turned away, but she could still see the moon-eyed panes, and all around her the air still seemed in motion—sluggish motion, as if heavy with swelling, creeping life. She breathed sharply, trying to shake off a sense of enclosure, restricting and suffocating. Seized by a sudden impulse,

150

she grabbed up a jacket from the chair, ran down the backstairs and out into the windy night.

The wind rushed to meet her with whispers of delight. It tugged and circled, walking her up the moonbright hillside towards the grove, attacking and retreating in soft rushes and breathless lulls. Nearer the grove, stronger now, it streamed her hair and swept the shadows from her mind. She sat in the grove for a long time, letting the pure wild force rush over her and then, feeling renewed and swept clean, she drifted back down the hill.

Strolling with the wind, she wended her way back down the slope, skirted the garden terrace, circled a thicket of young bay trees, and emerged on the front drive only a few feet from a rough rock wall.

On the windswept hillside she had forgotten about everything—about poor mad Margaret, about Miles, even about Paul, and she had forgotten entirely about the unfinished wing until suddenly she found that she was standing beside it.

She stared up at the rough wall that loomed above her head. Wind-driven shadows fled across the stone and dissolved into darkness. The torrent of air seemed to have grown colder, and the sound of it had changed from moan to shriek. As it grew in pitch and intensity, other sounds joined in—hissing whistles, staccato rattles, and a high-pitced keening drone. And then terror struck like a blow to the stomach, leaving her stunned and gasping. There was another sound. From somewhere inside the walls there issued a muffled, rhythmic thud that came and went and came again, like—hammering. Like someone using a hammer.

She ran, and the panic exploded into a flight of harpies that clawed and clung and choked her as she stumbled over the rough ground towards the north wing. At last the stones of the patio were under her feet, the dooryard. She burst through the door and collapsed on the kitchen floor.

The pain in her ankle was a wedge through which reality intruded. Shifting her position, she extended her left leg and examined it. The pain was diminishing and there was no sign of swelling, so it probably wasn't broken or even badly sprained. She couldn't remember doing it, but she must have turned it as she ran. Her heart was still racing, but in the familiar, well-lit kitchen, the panic was beginning to succumb. Rubbing the ankle, she considered the running and the panic.

The hammering could have been—undoubtedly was—nothing more than another wind noise. Something broken loose and flapping in the wind. The fact that it had seemed to come from inside the walls was undoubtedly due to imagination. Her imagination had conjured up a ghost. The ghost of a carpenter who could postpone the payment of his debt until his work was done; until he had finished the building of his ever-expanding kingdom. And then his heart had faltered and stopped in that awful room. An image appeared—a man, Calvin, sinking slowly to the floor, clutching his heart, his wildly rolling eyes seeking the shadows where something waited—something patient but inexorable.

Beth sighed. It really was discouraging to contemplate the way human beings insist on making sinister use of great gifts—like, for instance, using a

152

vivid imagination for the purpose of self-torment. She wondered what she was punishing herself for this time. Actually she really deserved it this time for being so supercilious about poor Margaret's delusions—forgetting how easily we are all deluded—how universally we pursue or flee from phantoms of our own devising. Well, she had fled all right, with such conviction that she had almost broken her leg. Smiling ruefully she staggered to her feet and, after first rather sheepishly locking the back door, limped around the kitchen readying it for the night. A little later she limped slowly up the back stairs, switched on the light in the bedroom—and in the space of a heartbeat the harpies were once again in full cry. Paul's bed was empty.

Without reason, without conscious thought, but with no hesitation, she started for the hallway in the old house where the closet door led to the unfinished wing. She went swiftly without any awareness of movement or surroundings, her mind an empty nightmare out of which familiar words echoed, "No, no, I'm sorry, I'm sorry. Paul. Paul where are you?"

She saw him immediately as she turned the corner in the upper hallway. He was standing in front of the narrow door, tensely alert, his small body rigidly erect. Relief flooded her eyes as she caught him up into her arms. His body felt stiff, unbending. With his hands on her shoulders, he held himself away, turning his face back towards the door. He seemed to be listening, his head cocked, eyes wide and unblinking.

The sound of the wind was muffled here in the center of the old house, a faint, distant moan, rising

153

and falling. But then nearer and more distinct there was once again a steady rhythmical beat. It stopped, began again, and then was gone.

"Paul," she whispered, and he turned to face her, his eyes enormous. "What is it? What is that noise, Paul?"

It took a moment for him to respond, for his huge eyes to lose some of their wild intensity and focus on her face, but then he frowned thoughtfully, biting his lip as if they were playing a guessing game.

"A hammer?" he asked.

"Oh, Paul!" she whispered and hugging him to her, she ran with him back towards the north wing.

154

17

" 'H E A V Y , heavy, heavy, hangs over thy head."

The winds had slackened, their swift ferocity tempered by a burden of heavy clouds. Bulging and ponderous, the gray clouds filed up over the horizon and gathered in great dark drifts, which slowly expanded to fill the entire sky. In the dim, silent calm, rational explanations took precedence very gradually, and the wave of horror ebbed; but it left behind it a sense of foreboding, a resigned expectation of new horrors to come. "Heavy, heavy, heavy, hangs over thy head," Beth wrote.

The writing had taken the form of a journal. She no longer considered sending the results to Warren. Warren had stopped writing, bored no doubt with a relationship whose physical manifestations were limited to pen and ink. The purpose of the journal was uncertain. It had become a kind of compulsion, perhaps only a nervous reflex to be indulged in at odd moments when the tight apprehensive alertness had reached a point where something had to be done. But it was also a search, a reaction to a growing feeling that there was something hidden, something absolutely vital that had somehow been kept from her. There were moments while she was writing, particularly when she had been at it for a long time and exhaustion had worn away the concentration needed for a planned and directed effort, when the answer seemed to be almost within her grasp. At such times she would write hurriedly, guiltily, as if expecting to be caught and punished.

"Heavy, heavy, heavy, hangs over thy head. What shall the owner do to redeem it? Step on a crack break your mother's back. The sky is falling said Chicken Little. The sky is falling."

Much of the writing was almost incoherent, increasingly childish—a self-indulgent jumble of bits and pieces of her life, fragmentary scenes, snatches of conversation, meaningless dregs from dreams, childhood games, patterns and rituals.

> "Mother mother I am sick. Call the doctor quick quick quick. Doctor doctor will I die? Yes my child but do not cry."

> I am ten years old now, and we are living near Los Angeles again. My little brother Andy is dead, and Wally is still living in Lancaster. I think Wally didn't want us to go away, but Bettina says that if she stays there in the house in Lancaster she will go mad. Her eyes are red and

swollen from crying. Wally sends us a little money, and we live in one half of a duplex in Burbank in the other half is a welfare mother with four children one of them is a baby. I have begun to have the chicken nightmare.

At first I dream it almost exactly the way it happened. I dream how I remembered about them while I was eating breakfast in the Hansens' kitchen. I sit very still my spoon halfway to my mouth dribbling milk. I think did I go back and turn them loose like I meant to? I must have but I can't remember. How long ago was it? How many days? I know it's been a long long time. I can't swallow the oatmeal that is in my mouth I get down from the chair and run and they shout after me Where are you going you haven't finished your breakfast.

The box is still in front of the doghouse and I'm afraid to move it. When I do there is the smell first and then I see them. They are lying on the clean straw that I'd put in the doghouse to make it nice for them. They are lying very still but I think maybe they are only unconscious and if I give them a drink pour water down their beaks maybe they will be all right again. I pick him up Robin the reddish one and his eyes are covered by papery eyelids and sunk back into his head and he feels flat and stiff and I drop him on the straw and

157

he is on his back now and something is moving on his chest. Little white worms are crawling into his chest.

And then the dream changes and the worms are grown fat and pink and turning into fingers—fat pink fingers are coming from Robin's chest and then I am running and the words are screaming inside me—no no I'm sorry I'm sorry I didn't mean for you to die.

Rock-a-bye baby in the tree top—Goddamn it Beth don't you see what you're doing?—What am I doing I'm not doing anything I only want to know what you think how you feel about it—That's exactly what I mean this is one thing you really have to decide for yourself. It's your body and your life that will be most affected—I know—there is a lump in my throat I feel frantic frustrated—I've thought and thought about how I feel but I need to know how you feel what you want me to do It's not fair for you to refuse to tell me. If you really don't want the baby and I have it, you might hate it later on—You decide Beth it's up to you—I'm frightened lost. How can I decide whether to have the baby if Jon won't tell me. There are so many things. It's way too soon almost two years before Jon can support us we'll have to borrow money but there is this baby who has already begun.

He doesn't help me but I don't decide

either I just keep putting off deciding until it's too late and then one day there is Paul but not because I decided and knew what I was doing.

Goddamn it Beth, don't you see what you're doing?—Why don't I Jon why don't I see what I'm doing?—Why didn't I that morning?—Jon is something the matter?—No nothing how many times must I say it Beth I'm just preoccupied something on my mind something I have to make up my mind about—Fright cold and quick—About us about us Jon? Is it about us?—No not about us I can't tell you what it's about—He is staring out the window again and I can't stand it—I can't stand it Jon—To tell you the truth neither can I this constant third degree about the state of my emotions leave my emotions alone Beth have a few of your own develop a little inner strength a little autonomy—My eyes are hot and dry—Nice words Jon real nice words but you don't mean them you don't really want me strong. You don't want me asking or telling or thinking or being not really. Not here or in bed either. What you want of me what I do for you that's not called strength Jon or autonomy either. There are other names for what I do for you—He just looks at me for a long time and the anger changes to something worse—Right you are Bethy. Dead on. Guilty as hell both of us mutual aiding

159

and abetting—He takes his coat off the couch—I'll be home late tonight—How late Jon?—Late—the door slams and I go to the window and watch him I watch him go for the last time.

Heavy, heavy, heavy, hangs over your head. Wee Willie Winkie runs through the town runs through runs in a nightgown.

There's been an accident Mrs. Corey. Your husband—No no accident, not Jonathan—Has your husband seemed depressed lately Mrs. Corey? Was he in bad health? Had you quarreled recently? Do you know any reason why your husband should have been on the coast highway at that time of night Mrs. Corey? Have you ever had a nervous breakdown Mrs. Corey? Weren't you under physchiatric care when you were still in school? Do you know any reason your husband might have wanted to take his own life? Why someone as healthy and successful and beautiful as your husband might want to take his own life? Can you think of any reason Mrs. Corey? No no reason. No reason. It was an accident. Don't you understand it had to be an accident it had to had to. Please please say it was an accident.

The first fall rain began in late September, and soon afterwards Miles showed up again at the Farm. He appeared one morning at breakfast, and just as before his presence was felt as a heightened tension, a sense of anxious expectancy. He seemed, however, to be in a particularly good mood, joking with Matthew, chatting about the flora and fauna of the high pastures with Rachel and Margaret, and even talking about ponies with Paul.

"I'm going to get a pony," Paul told him.

"Is that right? Who's going to get it for you, may I ask?"

"Eva. Eva is."

"Well, what do you know. A pony, huh? And what do you have to do—for the pony? Don't you have to do something to earn the pony? Most people have to do something very important in order to earn something as big as a pony."

Paul considered the question carefully. "I have to get older," he ventured, finally. "Just a little. Just a little older."

Miles turned his sharp grin on Beth. "And so we still have the city girl with us, too." he said. "Halfway expected to find you'd have gotten homesick for civilized life and flown the coop. Don't tell me you're turning into a farm girl? Developing an unexpected passion for country life, or something like that?"

You bastard, Beth thought. Careless about what the others might be thinking, even Eva, who was watching, hawklike; she glared at him.

"Nothing like that," she said coldly. "Unexpected passions usually turn out to be pretty insignificant, don't you think?"

The grin flared, sardonically appreciative, and Beth quickly looked down at her plate. She didn't want to accept anything from Miles, whether commendation or challenge. She only wanted him to leave her alone.

That night Beth locked the door to her bedroom and then lay awake for a long time, half expecting to hear the sound of a hand on the doorknob. But there was only the soft brush of rain at the windows and, from across the room, an occasional sleepy murmur from Paul, faint shadowy sounds that quickly blended with the quieting hush of the Farmhouse at night. After a while the locked door began to seem like an insult, a token of her lack of faith in her own resolve.

It was ridiculous, really. Crass as he was, she didn't really believe that Miles was a rapist, and nothing short of rape would be a threat—not now that she was forewarned and prepared. Getting out of bed she unlocked the door and soon afterwards fell asleep and slept undisturbed until dawn arrived, gray and dim. The rain had stopped, but dark clouds, low-slung and bulging, still filled the sky from horizon to horizon.

All day the clouds moved sluggishly across the sky, as though exhausted by their burden but unable to find release. Beth spent most of the day in her kitchen, polishing silver. She had asked Rachel for something useful to do, and had been given an enormous amount of tarnished silver. Most of it was extremely ornate and very old, dating back to the days when the O'Donnell family lived in the old house. It had obviously been unpolished for years and years, and the work was slow and tedious.

In the early afternoon Eva had gone to Pomo to take Oma to the doctor, a job that would probably have fallen to Matthew if he had been sober. Paul had gone with them, and Beth, too, had been asked if she wanted to go.

"We have just a few errands to run," Eva said. "Oma's appointment shouldn't take long, and then I have just a few things to pick up for Pete at Farmer's Supply." Beth had already begun to wash her hands, getting ready to go, when Paul said, "And we're going to get chickens, Umm. Baby ones." Beth turned quickly to Eva.

"I told Paul we'd pick up a dozen chicks for that old Plymouth Rock that's been brooding for so long," Eva said. "Might as well make some use of all that maternal instinct."

"It's the spotted one that goes——" Clucking peevishly, Paul waddled in a circle, arms spread wide.

Eva laughed. "Recognize her?" she asked Beth.

"I'm not very well acquainted at the chicken house, but I'm sure I will now, if we ever meet. But, you know, on second thought, I think I'd just as soon stay here and finish the silver. I'm not really in the mood for a long ride today."

Taking it out on the teapot, Beth polished furiously. She would have loved to have gone. There were a lot of things she needed to do in town. And what's more, she really should have gone, particularly if there were a good shrink in Pomo. She really was sick. How sick do you have to be to panic at the thought of a box of baby chicks, a box full of little, soft innocent balls of fluff? The angry self-disgust gradually dwindled and disappeared, to be replaced by the now familiar dull ache of apprehension. It was perhaps an hour later, and she was still sitting at the

163

kitchen table, the polishing cloth idle on the table before her, when she heard footsteps behind her, and turned to see Miles standing in the doorway.

There was a twinge of alarm, but also a kind of relief—a relief that the confrontation had arrived, and would soon be over and done with, and Miles would know what she was and what she was not.

"All alone?" he asked. "Thought maybe you'd gone to Pomo with the others."

"No. I decided against it. I felt like being alone." She looked at him pointedly. "All alone."

"I see. Well, in that case, I won't keep you—for very long." The grin again, slanted, insinuating, and then, "As I recall, you don't mind dispensing with the preliminaries."

"Get out," Beth said. She got to her feet, back against the wall. "Get out of here right now, or I'll start screaming."

"Go ahead, if you feel like it. You might find you enjoy it. I've known some who do. And you don't need to worry about disturbing anyone. There's only Dad and the ladies. Oh, if Dad hears you, he might want to come watch. He's a great one for watching. But, unfortunately, he's too smashed at the moment to move. And Grannie and Rachel won't mind. They've both done too much screaming themselves, in the past, to begrudge you a little."

Retreating against the sink, fear and revulsion thudding in her throat, Beth's eyes fell on the silver carving set, and then the knife was in her hand, and she held it out awkwardly, before her body.

"Good move." His eyes were gleaming, exultant. He moved towards her and then feinted and as her

164

hand came forward in response, his came down on her wrist. The knife fell to the floor. Pressing her back against the sink with his body, he bent her arm behind her and held it against the small of her back. His other hand was at the back of her neck, fingers gripping her skull. Tipping her head so she had to look at his face, he held her motionless. She struck wildly, ineffectively at his back with her free hand, struck again weakly, and then stood still. She had begun to feel him, his eyes, his body, as an overwhelming pressure, a terrible obliterating demand. And something huge and dark and hidden was answering the pressure, rushing up out of some deep place, killing her mind and will and leaving only an image—an image of something naked, cringing, a thing that crawled eagerly towards degradation and oblivion.

As if from a distance she heard his voice. "Aha, that's better. Don't want anyone to get hurt, do we? Now just hold still. Stand very still like a good girl." She felt his hands at her throat, unbuttoning her blouse and then behind her at the hooks of her bra. "No, don't look away. Just stand nice and quiet and look at me. That's a good girl. That's lovely. Fantastic." Her clothes were on the floor then at her feet and he moved against her, pressing her back again against the sink, the tiles cold on her bare skin, his hands hard on her body. Then he turned away, looking around the room, and released from his gaze, she tried weakly to move, to free her wrist from his grasp. But he turned back quickly, grasping her chin, forcing her eyes to meet his. "We're going upstairs, now," he said. "Might as well be comfortable."

165

When the shattering consuming violence was over and self-awareness began to return, he was standing beside the bed, pulling on his pants. Sprawled and naked, she lay perfectly still and watched him buckle his belt and pull on his boots, while the hatred washed up over her in great dark waves. Hatred for him, for the smug triumphant smile, for the satisfaction on his blotched and crooked face, but most of all for herself. The hatred burned in her throat, twisted her mouth, and scalded her eyes with tears.

Dressed now, he turned and looked down at her, and her loathing swam between them as if she were looking up at him through a pool of venom. After a moment his smile faded.

"Look," he said. "Don't blame yourself. You can't help it." The smile returned, self-mocking, now. "And neither can I, I suppose." He turned away, picking up his jacket, and then came back to the bed. "Look. Let me give you some advice. Take your kid and get out of here, while you still can. I know you probably think I'm just trying to make him lose out on the inheritance, but that's not it. What I'm trying to tell you is there are all kinds of ways of getting screwed, and some of them are worse than others, and you and the kid, especially the kid, are going to be in for one of the worst, if you hang around."

He stood looking down at her silently for a while longer, letting his eyes travel slowly down over her body, and then the slanted grin returned. "Or hang around, if you want to," he said. "Winter's pretty dull around her. I could use a little diversion, now and then."

166

18

THAT same afternoon Beth decided to leave Covenant Farm. The decision did not come easily, but once made and considered, the very agony of its birth became proof of its necessity. Why should it have been so difficult for her to arrive at so obvious a conclusion?—that for her and for Paul, no advantages, certainly no future inheritance, could outweigh the certain danger of staying longer at Covenant Farm. How could it possibly have taken her this long to see that the changes in herself as well as in Paul were for the worse? Paul's secretiveness and deviousness, his strange almost trancelike behavior, her own frightening hallucinations about the abandoned wing, and her inability to protect herself from Miles—all these things should have been clear warnings of the need to break whatever bond it was that had held her for so long. She would begin to make the arrangements at once, and they would leave as soon as it was possible.

Unfortunately the first step would have to be a confrontation with Eva. There would, now, have to be an accounting of the Farm's finances, and payment of the money that was due to Paul, one-fourth of the income since their arrival. It wouldn't be an easy thing to do. She hated having to ask, but the money was legally Paul's, and it was desperately needed. Without it, there would be no money to live on while they resettled in Los Angeles. Even more crucial was the amount necessary to pay for their trip home. So, she would ask immediately. Tonight at dinner she would ask Eva if they could have a private talk, and then she would ask about the money.

The rest of the day was a struggle against ever-increasing tension. Dinner was going to be a terrible ordeal, not only because of Miles' presence, but also because of the impending confrontation with Eva. As the afternoon crept by, Beth's courage and resolution waned, and she might have managed to rationalize a postponement of the talk with Eva, if it had not been for a vivid reminder that there was no time to lose.

It was not quite six, more than an hour before dinnertime, when she heard the sound of the van laboring on the last steep approach to the house, and she began to expect the momentary arrival of Paul, hungry and dirty and full of excitement about the trip to Pomo. But by seven, he still had not appeared.

Eva was in the dining room, helping Oma with the table, when Beth came in. No, Paul wasn't there. When they came back he had gone with Eva to take the chicks to the new mother in the hen house, but that had been almost an hour ago. "I told him to go right home and get cleaned up for dinner," Eva said.

168

"I'm afraid he was pretty grimy. He insisted on riding all the way home in the rear of the van so he could watch the chicks, and it's none too clean back there. Wherever he is, he's going to need some scrubbing before dinner. Have you looked on the patio?"

"No," Beth said. "But I will now." But there was another place where she would look first. As soon as the dining room door closed behind her, she began to run, up the front stairs and down the hall, around the corner—and he was there, standing in front of the closet door. Just as before, he seemed to be almost in a state of trance, somnambulant, his eyes fixed and staring, his body rigid in her arms. But this time, as she hurried towards the north wing, a strange snarling anger made her clutch him to her so fiercely that he began to whimper and struggle in her grasp.

Back in the north wing, she carried him directly to the bathroom and started the water running in the tub. Paul was not only dirty, but he smelled. A musty feathery smell that made her stomach shrivel and her throat tighten with fear. Stripping off his clothes, she sat him in the tub and splashed his face with water. He gasped, grinned up at her, and promptly flopped over on his stomach and began to blow bubbles in the water. Looking down at him, at the soft simplicity of his still babyish body, she was seized by an agony of love and anger, but now the anger seemed to be mostly at herself—for her own weaknesses. If she had been stronger, better, surely she could have protected him more from whatever it was that was reaching out for him, trying to make him a part of something strange and—evil. Yes, evil. She was sure of it.

169

"Look, Umm. I'm a whale. See how I'm a whale, Umm?"

"Paul. Why do you stand there in the hall by the closet door? What are you looking at?"

Paul stopped kicking and blowing and lay still in the water. After a moment he sat up and looked into her face. She returned the gaze, trying to let him see the urgency of the question and her love for him.

"Not looking," he said. "I was listening. When I stand there, it talks to me. Does it talk to you, Umm?"

"What does, Paul? What talks to you?"

He shrugged. "Somebody. Sometimes I have to go there." He turned his glowing, bath-wet face up to Beth, puckering his forehead in an exaggerated frown. "Why do I, Umm?"

There would be no further consideration of any kind of postponement. Eva would be told tonight, and then in the next day or two they would leave Covenant Farm forever. The strength of Beth's resolve served as a protective shield that helped her to get through dinner, helped her to suffer Miles' presence, even to speak to him briefly for the sake of appearances.

Miles was in a talkative mood, asking Eva and Paul about the trip to Pomo, and talking about his plans to build a stable near the ruins of the old barn, so that he could keep his favorite horse there, near the Farmhouse. "I spent a couple of hours down there today with Pete. It won't take much work to convert the grain shed into a couple of stalls and the old corrals are still in pretty good shape. Pete says he'll send Mike and Jim over tomorrow to get started on it. Shouldn't take more than a day or two."

Eva shrugged. "Well, it's all right with me, but I don't quite see the point, with all those empty stalls in the new barn."

"The point is, Tartar needs one hell of a lot of work, and if I keep him here I can ride him over every morning, instead of using the truck. Wear him down a little. Take some of the devil out of him."

"I'm afraid it will take more than that. Pete says that horse is a born renegade, And who's going to take care of him when you run off on one of your little pleasure jaunts? Carl isn't going to do it. I wouldn't let Carl get anywhere near that animal."

"Neither would I," Miles said. "Not anywhere near a horse as valuable as Tartar. No, when I go away, I'll take him back over to Pete's, Pete can handle him. The thing is, Ma, with a horse like Tartar you have to be at least as smart as he is."

Carl was staring at his plate. It was possible to hope that he had not heard or understood, but then he looked up and the hope was gone. "Besides," Miles went on, "I'll probably be around to take care of him myself for quite awhile now. Like I was telling Beth this afternoon, I'm kind of planning on putting a lot more effort into the Farm this year. Lot of things around here that could use a little extra attention."

"I see." Eva looked at Beth questioningly, but, like Carl, Beth lowered her head over her plate, fearing that if she looked at Miles her anger would burst out of her throat in a scream of rage.

Sometime later when she felt that she was once more in control of her voice, she asked Eva if she could talk to her briefly after dnner.

"Of course," Eva said. "I'll be working late in the

171

library. Why don't you just come on down anytime after you get Paul to bed?"

That night Beth read two stories to Paul before his eyes closed, and then waited several minutes longer to be sure that his breathing was deep and even, before she left the north wing and crossed through the old house to the library. Eva was sitting at the rolltop desk, a clutter of papers and record books spread out before her.

"Come in," she said. "I've just finished totaling things out for last month," she said, shaking her head and sighing. "Now what is it you wanted to discuss, my dear? Just pull up that chair and make yourself comfortable. I was about ready to take a cigarette break and rest a moment, so your timing is perfect."

Seated, Beth noticed that her hands had clutched each other as if for comfort. She separated them, firmly, only to have them immediately clutch the arms of the chair. Despairing, she concentrated on her thoughts, on producing in proper order the requests and announcements that she would have to make. "It's about the money, Paul's money," she began, and Eva took over.

"Yes, of course. We should have gotten around to this discussion a long time ago, but as you know I've been very busy, and then, too I must admit that I've been a little embarrassed about the state of our finances at the present. I guess I've been holding off, hoping things would improve and there'd be a little more favorable picture to present."

There was, it seemed, no money. According to the will, Paul was entitled to one-fourth of the net monthly income from all of the Farm's enterprises, but for the past several months there had been no profit at all. It had been necessary, in fact, for Eva to draw upon her own personal savings from time to time, in order to meet bills and payrolls. It was not anything to be too concerned about, nothing permanent or irrevocable. The Farm had been immensely profitable in the past and it would be again. It was just that there had been such a strange concurrence of unfortunate incidents since Lucien's death. Early in the summer, not long before Beth and Paul had arrived, there had been a forest fire that had wiped out a huge stand of timber that had been slated to supply the sawmill for the next several years. And then, right afterwards, an infestation of scabies had broken out in their largest flock of sheep. A great many sheep had to be destroyed and others had been quarantined until quite recently. Beth probably remembered some of the discussions about problems with veterinarians and inspectors, right after she arrived.

There really had been the most incredible string, almost a plague of calamities, but Eva had a feeling that they were over now. That the arrival of Beth and Paul had changed their luck and things would begin to pick up soon. And in the meantime, Eva would be glad to lend Beth a little money from her savings if there was something urgent, or even if she just felt the need of a little spending spree. "You've been pretty cooped up here the last few months," Eva said. "Maybe you'd enjoy taking a little private trip into Pomo someday soon. Or even up to Eureka. We could take care of Paul for you while you're gone, and you could just indulge yourself a little. Stay at a nice

173

hotel, buy some pretty things."

"No," Beth said. "That's not—I wouldn't care about the money, except that . . ." To strengthen her resolve she conjured the image of Paul before the closet door, entranced, rigid. "I've decided not to stay. I think—I really want to take Paul and go back to Los Angeles. I know it will mean that he will lose the inheritance, and maybe that will be all for the best, for everyone concerned. Maybe—" She stopped, her voice strangled by sudden fear. For a fleeting moment it seemed that Eva's face was transforming, the lines hardening, contorting into a mask of rage. But then, suddenly, she was smiling again.

But why would Beth want to do something so drastic, so foolish? If something was wrong, if she had complaints, surely they could be discussed, adjustments could be made, problems ironed out. Eva's voice was measured, reasonable. It was only natural that it should be a little difficult for Beth to make such a drastic change in her life, and she mustn't think that the family, all of them, didn't appreciate the sacrifices she had made. But she must think of the others, too. Think what it would mean to Margaret and Rachel to lose Paul now, after they had grown to love him.

"And to me as well," Eva said. "I really don't think you realize what Paul means to me. To me and to Lucien and Calvin."

"Lucien and Calvin?" Beth said, aghast.

"Yes, what it would have meant to them to have Paul here," Eva said smoothly. "What it would have meant if they could have known that Paul would grow up here, just as Lucien and I did, and that someday

174

the farm, all of Covenant Farm, would be his."

There was a passion in Eva's eyes that reached out to Beth, swept around and over her, so that she had to push her way through it, groping blindly for the sure ground of her resolve. "I know," she said. "I know and I'm terribly sorry. It's just that I've been feeling lately that it's not good for Paul and me here—that there are forces, pressures that are not good for us."

Something hardened again in Eva's face. "Miles said something about talking to you this afternoon. Was it something he said? Did he tell you—something, or do something, that made you uneasy?"

"No. No, not really. It wasn't just what he said. I've just been feeling that Paul"—Beth steeled herself—"that Paul is in some kind of danger here."

"Danger, nonsense," Eva's response was not surprise or concern but immediate denial. "Nonsense. How could Paul be in any danger here where he is so much loved? So important to all of us?" She leaned forward and put her hand over Beth's and held it firmly. "Beth," she said, "you can't leave. Paul is a Corey. The Farm is his responsibility, his birthright. And you are a part of it, too, now. A part of the family. It is your destiny now, too, just as it is Paul's. I'm sure you feel that, understand that. Just as you understood Jonathan. Understood his special gifts and needs. You will come to understand all of us here, all the family, and that your destiny is here among us."

Eva's voice, deeply calm, soothing, flowed over Beth, and reason struggled weakly against an overpowering urge to yield, to relax and leave everything to Eva, to Eva and the family. But then the image of the entranced Paul returned and Beth clung to it desperately. "No," she said. "No, we have to go. We have to leave as soon as we can."

"Well then," Eva's voice was still entirely calm, but colder now, matter of fact. "If we can't change your mind, I suppose we'll have to let you go." She leaned back in her chair, legs crossed, lighting a cigarette. Shaking out the match she tossed it in the wastebasket and sat back scrutinizing Beth through eyes narrowed against the smoke. She seemed relaxed, resigned, but something still fluttered in Beth's throat interfering with her breathing. At last Eva said, "I'll be going to Pomo again in a week or so and you can go with me and we'll see about getting your tickets. And we'll get enough money to see you through for a little while until you can get settled again in Los Angeles. I'll just take a little more out of my savings, and you can pay me back someday when it's convenient." She smiled warmly. "We'll take care of everything. And in the meantime, we'll just concentrate on enjoying you and Paul for at least a few more days. Perhaps it will be best if we don't tell the others right away. Let them go on enjoying having you here, instead of grieving over the future."

Relief flooded over Beth. Eva was being so reasonable and so kind, lending them money and taking care of everything. Eva was taking care of everything, and in just a few more days they would be on their way to Los Angeles. Back in the north wing Paul was sleeping peacefully, flat on his back with arms outflung, pink fingers curled over parchment palms.

"We're going away," Beth told him silently, "in just a few more days."

19

S H E was walking along a country road. It was a warm, green day and the air smelled of spring. She was barefooted, barelegged, her body slight and supple under a flowered cotton dress that swung short and full from a smocked yoke. The air was cool on her skin, but under her bare feet the dust was warm and powdery. She felt free, unbound, bouyant with a pure bubbling joy that had nothing to do with any expectation, but only with the air and the sun and the pleasure of moving free and coltlike under the short dress.

She began to skip, knees high, hair bouncing on the back of her neck. She skipped high and light, barely feeling the earth under her feet. And then, without any warning, not even a sudden cold wind or darkening sky, a shattering force caught her, flung her violently, twisting and grasping, across the grass and into the barbed wire of the fence that ran beside the road. There was a dark confusion of pain and blood, and then she was back again walking beside the road, but now she was crying. The tears were bitter, bewildered, and yet it was as if she had somehow expected and acquiesced in what had happened. As if she knew she had somehow invited the force, and the barbed fence, and the pain.

She walked along, head down, crying and watching the blood that ran down her leg and dropped onto the dust of the road. And then the drops of blood were becoming larger and larger and swelling into great oozing bubbles, and the bubbles grew and became transparent, so that she could see something moving inside them, squirming, bulging the bubble walls. One of the bubbles had become enormous, and something was moving violently inside it, pushing at the bubble wall, trying to get out. The wall bulged, and as she watched, terrified, unable to run or look away, the protrusion grew, elongated, and broke open, and something pushed its way out—a three-toed claw, orange-red, the foot of a chicken.

And then she was running, screaming terrible throat-rending sounds, while inside her head the words echoed, "No, no. I'm sorry. I'm sorry. I didn't mean for you to die."

She awoke sitting upright in bed, shaking, drenched with sweat. The realization came quickly, the wonderful relief that follows awakening from a nightmare—the blessed knowledge that it was only a dream, it wasn't real, it didn't really happen. But this time the relief was short-lived. This time it was followed almost immediately by a realization that was almost as frightening as the dream itself: the chicken dream had returned.

In all the weeks since she had been at Covenant Farm, she had not had the dream, not even once. Not even in these last few weeks since she had become so uneasy, so fearful for Paul as well as for herself. And now when she had made the decision to go away, the dream had returned. Why should it come back now? What did it mean?

The next day everything was much the same as it had been before, as was the next day and the next. Except that now Beth was trying to keep Paul within sight every moment. She had begun to teach him the alphabet, and she spent hours sitting with him at the kitchen table while he traced large wobbly letters or drew sausage ponies with toothpick legs galloping across sheets of wrapping paper. When he wanted to go outside to play, she went with him and sat nearby reading while he pushed a wheelbarrow around the patio, or built a tepee of grape stakes in the garden. Most of the time Paul seemed content to have her with him, but now and then he grew restless and distant, and she would catch him listening, his head tipped to one side. Once or twice he tried to talk her into letting him go. "I'm going to go play now, Umm. Not you. You stay here."

"No, Paul, You can't. Stay here with me."

"I have to. I have to go"—a pause, eyes rolling thoughtfully—"I have to go look for Rufus. I have to ask Rufus if he wants this cookie." He pulled a disintegrating fragment that might once have been related to a cookie from his jacket pocket.

179

"All right. I'll go with you. We'll both go look for Rufus."

She got up, but Paul stood still, straddle-legged, staring up at her from under his brows—a dark, hidden look so unlike him in its duplicity that Beth was startled, almost frightened. Stooping she took his face in her hands, forcing him to meet her eyes. But he jerked away, and a little later she caught him trying to sneak away.

As time passed, the constant alert watchfulness took its toll. With each day Beth felt more exhausted, and with the exhaustion came a growing sense of urgency, as if time were running out. She was very tired, time was running out, and there was always the vague gnawing awareness of something of vital importance that fled before her whichever way she turned—something almost visible, almost tangible but not quite.

Dinner every night with the whole family was much the same as ever. No one mentioned the impending departure. Beth had understood and appreciated Eva's decision to wait until the time had almost come before telling the others, so that there would be less time for tearful scenes, and possibly arguments and accusations. But surely now the time must be very close, and still no one seemed to know. No one that is except Paul. It was on the third night after Beth's interview with Eva that Paul suddenly asked, "We're not going away, are we, Umm? We're not, huh, Umm? Are we?"

She pulled his pajama top over his head, hiding his anxious gaze, giving herself a moment to think. But when his face emerged, framed now by a fringe of tawny hair, it was still anxious, questioning. "Are we, Umm?"

"Who told you we were going away? Was it Eva?"

"No. Not Eva."

"Who was it then?"

He opened his mouth, reconsidered, and closed it again. Chin tucked, he looked up at Beth sideways, and then offered tentatively, "Somebody."

She sighed. "All right, somebody," she said impatiently. "And somebody is right. You and I are going to go home—to Los Angeles."

She had known that Paul would be unhappy about leaving, but she was not prepared for his reaction. "No, no," he wailed, enormous tears springing from his eyes. Splashing down his cheeks, they were almost immediately dripping off his round chin, dampening his pajamas.

"I don't want to," he sobbed. "I don't want to go away," and then, "I can't. I can't go."

"Yes, you can. We both can go back to Los Angeles and live just like we did before."

"No, no." Paul was almost screaming. "I can't. I'm not supposed to. I have to stay here always and always."

"Why, Paul?" He would have turned away, but she held him by both shoulders and shook him sharply. "Why can't you go? Tell me. Why can't you go away?"

Trapped, unable to escape her gaze, Paul's eyes met hers, but suddenly they were no longer Paul's. Where there had always been the wide, unqualified welcome, even beneath tears or anger, there was now a veil, a perverse, guarded darkness. As Beth stared,

181

he twitched his shoulders out of her grasp and covered his face with both hands. Fighting back an apprehension that was almost fear, Beth pulled his hands away and exposed a tear-glistened mask, blankly innocent. "Because of the pony?" he said with the lifting inflection that made so many of his utterances both statement and question. "I can't go because of the pony?"

"Oh, Paul, there isn't any pony. Not yet. And Eva hasn't said when you could have one. She may not mean soon."

"No. No. Right away. The pony's coming right away."

"I don't think so. I'll tell you what, Paul. When we get back to Los Angeles, I'll find a place where you can ride a pony, and we'll go there every weekend. And then, someday when we've gotten settled, we'll look for a stable someplace nearby where you can keep a pony, and then we'll get you one of your very own." She rushed on, forcing enthusiasm, while Paul's eyes stared, wide and dark, reading, she felt sure, her own mistrust of what she was saying. He climbed into bed then and turned his face to the wall, and when she asked him if he wanted a story, he said, "No. No more story."

20

A week had passed since she had told Eva, and except
for the return of the chicken dream, nothing had
changed. There had been no further mention of
Beth's intentions, or of the trip to Pomo that Eva had
said must be the necessary first step. And Beth had
been unable to find another opportunity to talk to Eva
alone. Whether or not by intention, Eva had been
arriving late to dinner and leaving early, and twice
when Beth had asked to speak to her privately, there
had been some reason for postponement. Eva was too
busy just then, or not feeling well. And when in
desperation, Beth had asked at the dinner table if Eva
was planning another trip to Pomo soon, she had only
agreed that, yes, a trip would be necessary before too
long.

"Why," Eva's smile was calm, undecipherable, "did
you want to go along this time?" leaving Beth to
wonder if she could possibly have forgotten their dis-

cussion and the promises she had made; or if she were challenging Beth to state her reasons there, publicly, and thereby assume responsibility for the ensuing grief and trauma. If that had been her intention, her ruse worked. Beth had not had the courage to call her bluff.

There were, Beth realized, other, more desperate measures that could be taken. She could pack their things and demand to be driven immediately to Sturmville. But what would they do then without money or transportation? Terrifying scenarios presented themselves, alone with a frightened, hungry Paul, threatening strangers, darkness, rain. She would wait, she decided, just a little longer, for Eva to fulfill her promises.

She was writing now every night—a desperate and often ineffective defense against insomnia and nightmares. In spite of the writing, the chicken dream returned. She awoke shuddering and gasping and reached for her journal.

This time it started with a picnic. Paul with me on a sunny hillside. Paul picking flowers running here and there exclaiming laughing. I'm lying in the sun warm contented. Paul's voice—Come here Umm come and see—to a hillside and a dark cave and then in the cave somewhere deep down and all around us bats flying tiny squeaky shadows. Paul is frightened. Trying to comfort him speaking calmly fighting against what is coming. Fighting against the fear ballooning exploding wip-

184

ing out reason shreiking with my voice because the bats have grown and the air is full of their heavy bodies their squawking cries the rank rotten chicken smell of death. Death smell and feathers thick smothering throat-clogging. Someone— Paul Paul choking gasping for air.

The sky is falling. Your house is on fire your children will burn. Forgive us our trespasses if I should die before I wake forgive us our trespasses.

But sometimes the writing helped, and in the day-time everything remained much the same as before. Matthew had emerged from wherever he hid himself when he was drinking heavily and returned, shaky and bloated, to the evening gatherings in the dining room. Miles, too, was very much in evidence—not only at the evening meal, but also sometimes during the day, in the valley near the old barnyard, on his red horse. Tartar was stabled now in his new accommodations, and in the mornings Miles rode him across the hills to the new barnyard. But sometimes he came back early to train the horse on the level ground of the valley floor near the ruins of the old barn. Beth was careful to be aware of his whereabouts in order to avoid a chance meeting, but one day she stood with Paul at the edge of the patio and looked down the hill to where he was working the horse, riding him around and around in a tight figure eight. Paul was entranced, and Beth knew she would have been too, by the rider's skill and the horse's beauty, if the rider had been anyone but Miles.

He rode well, relaxed and perfectly balanced, holding the huge horse to a slow controlled gallop. Tightly checked, neck arched, tail pluming in the wind, Tartar moved high and smooth in a tense rhythmic pattern. He would have seemed a beautiful machine, unalterably responsive to rein and heel, if it had not been for the gaping mouth and the furious white-rimmed eyes. But then, as they watched, he stumbled and broke his gait, and the heavy quirt in Miles' hand rose and fell again and again, and Tartar reared and plunged, snorting and squealing.

Paul's face was taut with shock. "Why is he hurting him? Why is he hurting Tartar? Make him stop it, Umm."

Shaken herself by the violence of the scene and by Paul's reaction, Beth turned and almost ran towards the house, dragging Paul after her.

That night, hoping to catch Eva alone to demand that a date be set for the trip to Pomo, Beth arrived early in the dining room. The table was set and a fire was burning in the fireplace, but there was no one in the room. Beth went to stand in front of the fire, while Paul pranced, pony fashion, around the table. He circled the table several times and then, announcing that he was going to go help Oma, he disappeared into the kitchen. And it was only a moment later that Miles appeared in the doorway. Beth started towards the kitchen, but Miles moved quickly, blocking her path, and she retreated back towards the fireplace.

"Relax," he said. "You're in no danger. I never indulge on an empty stomach. Besides, it's not going to be very private in here in a few minutes. We wouldn't want to be hard at it when the ladies arrive, now would we?"

He moved slowly, gently, as if to avoid spooking a timid horse, until he was standing beside her. His back to the fire, he relaxed, smiling his bony smile. She stood her ground, her hands clenched into fists behind her back.

"Nice to see you," he said, polite, impersonal. "Always nice to see you. Have to drop over again soon, make another little social call."

Without looking at him Beth whispered, "I despise you."

He chuckled. "I'm aware of that. That's part of your charm, as a matter of fact. But I notice you haven't taken my advice—to get the hell out of here."

"I've tried. I am trying. I've told Eva that we're going."

"You did? Well, that may have been your first mistake. And she said . . . ?"

"She agreed. She's going to take me to Pomo soon to make the arrangements."

"I see. Look, don't you have anyone, any friends or family who might come and get you?"

"No. Not really. There was someone, but he's stopped writing."

"Or you've stopped getting his letters. Do you still walk to the mailbox?"

"No. I haven't lately. Eva's been taking my mail down for me."

He shook his head. "And you really think your boyfriend's been getting them? You really do ask for it, you know."

187

Forgetting to keep her eyes averted, Beth stared at Miles. "You mean you really think she'd take my letters?"

"Look, I tried to tell you about my dear mum when we first met. Stealing your letters would be nothing. A warm-up exercise." The light sardonic tone was suddenly laced by honest hatred, harsh and acrid.

Wonder and something almost like pity stirred somewhere beneath the fear and anger. "You really hate her, don't you?" she asked.

He turned to look at her. "Yeah," he said without grinning. "It's mutual."

"Why?"

"Why does she hate me? You might say it's my legacy from my old man. She hated him first. When I was born, she hated me on sight."

"And Carl?" Beth said. "She doesn't hate Carl."

"Right." He was grinning again. "Perhaps this is a good time for another bit of family history. Matthew isn't Carl's father. And who is, you might ask? The one great love of my dear mother's life, the beautiful, incomparable Lucien. That's right, her brother. Does that shock you? Yeah, obviously it does. Good. A few more shocks, and you might get serious about clearing out of here. Real serious. Because otherwise, you're never going to make it."

"But why would she want to keep us here against our will? Why does it matter that much to her?" But as she asked an answer intruded, a wildly insane answer, but no more insane than some others that were beginning to seem possible. "Is it because of the covenant?"

"The covenant? Ahah. You *are* beginning to get

into the scene, aren't you. Who told you about the covenant?"

"Margaret. Margaret told me about it, but I thought it was just—"

"Senility? Yeah, well maybe. But she's not the only one."

"Who—?"

"Well, there's Matthew for one. He believes it. He didn't at first, but I guess you might say he was converted. By a logging truck, among other things. Forcefully persuaded, you might say."

"And Eva?"

"Does she believe that Calvin had some kind of special arrangement with the Old Nick? Yeah, I think she believes it. I don't think she'd admit it, but she believes it, all right."

"And how about you?"

"Me? Hell, no, I don't believe it. My sins are for my own enjoyment. I don't believe in dedicating them to anybody or anything. Besides, I figure I got left out of the bargain entirely. I don't get the land, and I sure as hell didn't get the infernal beauty. I did get something though, just a bit of the unholy power, don't you agree?" He chuckled. "Shouldn't grudge me that. Where would I be without it, with this face."

Beth was staring at him, thinking nothing more coherent than a vague jumble of doubts about his sanity, or her own, or both; but he must have read something else in the denial and aversion on her face, because suddenly his grin hardened into a snarl. "Now, you take Jonathan," he said. "He got it all. All the land, the looks, *and* the power. Oh yes, he had the power all right. Chucked up the land and the money,

189

but he couldn't get away from the power, could he? Found himself a little woman just begging to be tyrannized. Must have really turned you on, old Jonathan. You two get into chains and whips, that kind of thing?"

Beth turned to flee, but he caught her wrist and jerked her back, and at that moment the kitchen door opened admitting Oma carrying a steaming bowl, and Paul trotting behind her. And at almost the same instant there were voices in the hall, and Eva came in followed by Matthew supporting Margaret.

Beth looked down at her wrist, still in Miles' fist, and then up at his face. The angry grin was gone. "Look," he said, quietly, under cover of the chattering voices. "I'll help you. I'll drive you and the kid into Pomo. But we'll have to talk about it later."

21

I T was very late, almost three in the morning, and Beth still hadn't slept. Across the room in his cot Paul, too, seemed restless, tossing and turning and making strange noises in his sleep. Staring into the darkness, her eyes wide as the lidless eyes of a painted doll, she had gone over everything a thousand times. The past, all the events since her arrival at the Farm; the present, the incredible conversation with Miles in the dining room; and the future, the courses of action left open to her tomorrow or as soon as possible.

If she accepted Miles' premise that Eva was insane, and she was beginning to see that there was good reason to do so, there was no time to waste. She and Paul had to leave immediately, even if they had to start out walking and hitchhike all the way to Los Angeles. Or there was Miles' offer of a ride to Pomo, but that meant there must be a meeting to make arrangements. A secret meeting, since it was only too obvious that Miles did not want Eva to know he had been involved. The thought of a secret meeting with Miles was another horror—but no other possibilities remained. There was no other source of help. She saw that with absolute clarity. She understood now that if Miles were afraid to help openly, the others were all very much more afraid. She pictured herself asking, and saw with the vividness of a vision how Matthew would only snigger as he went to tell Eva, how Rachel would turn away, resigned and hopeless beyond pity or concern; and how Oma would listen in growing panic, her eyes turned away looking desperately for Eva's instructions.

As the dark hours crawled by, Beth came to the realization not only that she was trapped, but that she had been almost from the moment she arrived at Covenant Farm. With no means of transportation, no telephone, no money, her mail intercepted, how could she have gotten away. Earlier, before Eva had reason to suspect her of wanting to leave, she might have managed to walk away, but now even that might be impossible. There were, she now knew, people who would come after her. People who would have no compunction about how it was done.

Half asleep, dream mixing with reality, she tried to picture it—she and Paul on foot with no money or exact destination, fearful of pursuit. She pictured herself and Paul scrambling up barren hillsides, pursued by a thundering posse of Jaspers, or by Matthew and Carl—Carl who was not good with little things, and Matthew who might set Carl on them and then watch, like a cruel boy sicking his dog on a cornered cat. I can't, I can't, she thought, and suddenly she was overcome by a paralyzing weariness, a great lethargic urge to relax and submit. To submit to Eva, to Miles, to the covenant—the thought was horrifying but at the same time compellingly seductive—if it weren't for Paul. She would never be able to relax, submit, escape into oblivion because of Paul, and for a moment she resented him—hated him.

My God, I'm crazy. Crazy! she thought. What's the matter with me? Forcing herself to a sitting position, she reached for the light and then sat panting, staring around the room, trying to saturate her senses with the solid three-dimensional facts of her surroundings—the foot of the bed, Paul in his cot, the dresser. Her eyes fell on her journal on the bed table, and snatching it up, she opened it and began to write feverishly.

> The sky has fallen. Everyone here is mad. Margaret is certainly and Eva, perhaps everyone. Everyone believes that a long time ago Calvin Corey bargained with the devil for wealth and power and Margaret's beauty and that he was permitted to postpone the payment of his debt until his work was done and until there was no one, no Corey heir, to carry on the pact. I don't believe that of course— no sane person could—except that Paul talks to someone I don't see and there's hammering in the unfinished wing and a room that is full of terror because someone died there, someone who was ter-

ribly afraid of what would come after. Oh my God forgive us our trespasses if I should die before I wake and they all lived happily ever after now go to sleep Paul and quit making noises. I've hardly slept all night I'm not going to get you up again you're Bettina's baby not mine and you should be in her room bothering her except Wally's in there and they're doing things they don't want you to see. You're doing it again making funny noises like a chicken like a little chicken with a piece of grain stuck in its throat. I'm getting angry you can just stop it Andy because I'm not going to get up again. The noises stop and then I'm waking up and it's light already and I have to go to the bathroom and Andy is in his crib lying on his face with one of his hands with its fat pink fingers sticking out through the bars and I take hold of it and the fingers are stiff and cold and his eyes are stiff too and papery and I'm screaming and screaming and running running running into pain and darkness.

She was crying, choking tears streaming down her face, her nose running. She covered her face with the bedspread, stifling the sobs that were like explosions in her throat and lungs. Shaking, rocking back and forth, she cried and cried, and she knew that she was nine years old, that she was still nine years old and there were parts of her that had always been nine years old because she had killed her little brother, had heard him choking and let him die, and God would never forgive her, except she was only nine years old and she hadn't meant to, and never meant to, never meant to do anything wrong, and never would again, not ever.

After a long time everything ran out. She was lying on the bed on top of the covers and she was limp and exhausted and her throat ached from the crying. And then she went to sleep.

22

AWAKENING early in the empty silence of predawn, Beth accepted level after level of revelation, and with each revelation there were new depths of pain. Now that the barrier had been broken, she was besieged by memories. All the details, all the images and echoes, had begun to rise up now, one after the other, through the years of forgetting. She remembered now how Bettina had shrieked and sobbed, screamed terrible things. She remembered backing away, holding up her arms against the stabbing words. "You must have heard him. You let him die. You were jealous of him, jealous. You let him die. You let him die." And she remembered her own screaming so vividly that her ears rang with it, remembered running, running away blindly down the stairs and out onto the sidewalk and street, running, running, her nightgown tangling, tripping, Wally running after her, shouting her name. And then a car from nowhere with gaping faces—and the quick hard blow that she said yes to, yes to the pain, and to the darkness, yes yes yes.

The hospital came back, faint and fragmented, white walls, a fat nurse with a kind face, sleeping and waking and sleeping again, drugged probably. And then no more until bits and pieces of the long ride to Camp Tyler, and then clearer memories of the camp and coming home again, but no more about Andy. No more ever about Andy, except the knowledge that he had died of pneumonia while she was away—a knowledge, she now realized, that had always been carefully unexplored, untampered with.

And no one ever told her differently. Bettina wouldn't have. Bettina, who had always avoided realities, had probably seen Beth's forgetting as a blessing. And by the time Beth had first consulted the psychologist, during that awful first year at college, Bettina was dead. Wally had gone away somewhere, and there was no one who remembered about Andy and how he had died.

How had he died? Beth had read several times in recent years about sudden crib death, always with strangely violent feelings of empathetic grief. But she had not remembered. And because she had not, could not, remember, what had she done? What had she done to herself, and, undoubtedly, to Paul?

The possibilities were endless and endlessly painful. One more than all the rest because it was irrevocable. It was forever too late to change what she had done to Jonathan, but someday she would have to know. Someday she would have to ask the questions about guilt and punishment, love and pain. About the need to escape accountability that had made her seek bondage, total submission to the enthralling seductive authority that had been, for Jonathan, only too easy and far too absolute. And she would have to know if she had been, for Jonathan, a constant tantalizing invitation to the kind of wanton power that he had tried so desperately to leave behind when he had run away from Covenant Farm, and perhaps from life.

The pain of those questions was yet to come, and Beth found that for now she was able to accept her new knowledge with a sad resignation that was quite different from panicky flight and denial of the past. The truth was that at the moment there were other things, no less terrible, but much more urgent to be faced.

There was Eva, an Eva insane enough to steal letters, to lie and connive and perhaps resort to even greater evils in order to keep Paul at Covenant Farm. And there was also Miles, who might or might not be sincere about helping them get away. There was at least a chance that he really intended to help. She had no illusions about his motives. If he helped them it would be because it suited his own purposes to do so. But whatever his motives, if Miles would help them, could be induced to help them, she would do whatever was necessary, face whatever had to be faced.

The half-light of dawn had thinned almost imperceptibly into the dull gray of a heavily overcast day. Beth got out of bed and, going to the mirror, stared at her own reflection, trying to see the person she had been, and might have been, and might possibly become, now that she might be free to grow and change. But the face that stared back seemed unchanged, Beth's face but, as always, Bettina's also. The slender neck, heavy hair, the fragile line from cheek to chin, gifts of Bettina's genes—and the eyes—fearful, propitiatory, tear-haunted—the crazy eyes that had seduced Jon, a legacy also. It was not a face for conflict, particularly when the opposing forces were so powerful. First there would be Miles.

From the mirror she went to the window and looked out over the greenhouse to where the hill dropped away to the old barnyard. Miles should be crossing the patio soon on his way down to Tartar's stable. If she and Paul happened to be out in the patio . . . A very short time later she shepherded a groggy, grumpy Paul out onto the clammy stones of the patio. Pulling him out of bed, she had had him half-dressed before he was fully awake, bundled him into his coat, planted his hobby horse in his hand, and led him out onto the patio.

"Come on, Paul. Don't you want to play outdoors? You always like to play outdoors."

"Not now," Paul whimpered. "Now I want some hot chocolate. I want to play outdoors when it's morning."

"This is morning, Paul. It's just dark because it's cloudy. And we'll have some hot chocolate later. If we're going to play outdoors at all today, we have to now, before it starts to rain. Come on, get on your hobby horse and let's go over and look at Tartar."

Paul brightened. Not even such a well-justified case of grouchiness was proof against the lure of the great bronze horse. Straddling his hobby horse, he cantered eastward towards the place where the terrace ended, above the valley. Beth hurried after him, slipping now and then on the wet stones.

"There he is. There's Tartar." Paul had reached the edge of the patio, and as Beth came up beside him, she saw that Miles' horse was, indeed, still in his corral. Miles should be appearing soon.

"Hello, Tartar," Paul called, waving. The waving fingers moved slower and slower and stopped as Paul, forgetting even to lower his arm, sank into a rapture of enthralled attention. Beth, too, felt herself caught up—hypnotized almost as thoroughly as Paul by the incredible beauty and power of the enormous animal.

Tartar was pacing his corral. His thick neck bowed in a graceful arch, tail pluming, great corded muscles sliding under the gleaming hide, he charged the corners of his prison, whirled, retraced his steps and charged again. After a few minutes Paul began to pace back and forth along the edge of the patio. Timing his turns to those of the horse, he pranced and turned, clutching the hobbyhorse's reins. A door slammed in the distance, and Beth turned to see Miles crossing the patio. He moved towards her, smiling his thin white smile.

"Well, well. We are up and about early today, aren't we? Maybe we'll make a good country girl out of you after all."

Stiff-faced, Beth said, "Did you mean it when you said you'd help us get away? Will you drive us to Pomo?"

Without turning his head, Miles flicked his eyes towards the house. "Sure," he said. "I meant it. But we'll have to be cagey. If Eva gets wind of it, neither one of us is going to get anywhere."

"Well, how can we—"

"I've got a few things to work out. Plans to make. We'll talk it over tonight after everyone's asleep. Safer that way. Around eleven, your parlor. You remember the spot, I'm sure. Don't forget to leave the door unlocked." Without waiting for a response, he went on down the hill towards Tartar's corral.

She had expected it, had tried to prepare herself for the fact that Miles would not agree to help them without some kind of extortion. If she locked the door or by some miracle managed to resist him successfully, it was quite likely, given his need for conquest, that he would refuse to help. She smiled bitterly. And so what? It wasn't as if she had virtues of any description left to protect. And this time she might even escape some of the self-loathing by telling herself that it had been for Paul.

The day was a torment. Paul, restless and alert, seemed to be continually expecting something. It was necessary to watch him constantly, never relaxing her vigil even for a moment. Time and again she hoped fervently that whatever Miles was planning would happen quickly. She wouldn't be able to bear the strain much longer. If only she could be sure that, after she had paid his ransom, he would agree to carry out his plan immediately. But at least it would not be long until she knew.

At last the cloud-dimmed day darkened into night. The evening meal, an agony of careful pretense, was endured, and Beth returned to the north wing. For almost an hour Paul tossed and mumbled fitfully and then slept deeply and peacefully. A little before eleven, Beth went down to the parlor.

201

She waited. The windless night seemed full of small sounds and movements, uncertain but insistent. Sitting stiffly on the edge of a chair, she was aware of enclosing darkness, the darkness of Calvin's castle, of the greedy, possessive tyranny of the surrounding walls. That these dark walls had once masqueraded as a refuge, a place of sanctuary, now seemed incredible.

At last, one of the uncertain sounds repeated itself, became louder, became footsteps, and the door opened. Miles came in quickly. In the dim light his hatchet face was pale and sharp. Closing the door to a narrow crack, he listened carefully for a long time. At last he relaxed, and his jeering grin blazed.

"Thought I heard something," he said.

"The house makes noises," she told him.

"So I've been told. Now me, I've never heard anything that couldn't have been made by natural causes. Squirrels in the attic, prowling relatives—depends what you're listening for. Like just now—I thought I might have heard a prowling relative, but I guess not."

There was no point in trying to explain to him about the surrounding walls—or the beat of hammers in the unfinished wing. "Will you help us get away?" she asked. "Will you lend me enough money for bus tickets?"

Moving deliberately, Miles settled himself on the couch, took a package of cigarettes from his pocket, lit one, inhaled, and then leaned forward to toss the match in the direction of the fireplace. His measured movements and exaggerated calm might have been construed as an attempt to relax the tension, to reas-

202

sure, if it had not been for the slight involuntary twitching of the muscles around his eyes and mouth—like those of a cat watching the wounded crawl of a captive mouse. It was obvious that he was relishing the situation, savoring this moment that put her, more than ever, completely at his mercy.

"Relax," he said at last. "It's all arranged. I made some calls today. Friend of mine's going to arrange an emergency at the logging camp, one that I'll have to take care of. Tomorrow morning I'll go on over to the barnyard as usual, but then Pete will get a call and he'll have to drive me back here to get the van and my gear. There'll be a lot of rushing around getting the van loaded—some new motor parts, tools and so forth. You all be ready. When you hear Pete's truck, you take the kid and start up the hill. Get into the trees as soon as you can, in case someone should happen to look up that way. But if all goes well, everyone will be too busy with Pete and me to check on you for a while. Go over the hill and on down to the old town. If you follow the road through the town it'll take you down to the highway. There's an old shed right by the gate. Stay in the shed till I come along. After I let you off in Pomo, I'll go on up to the camp and stay there for a day or two before I come back, and nobody will suspect a thing. You can catch the bus in Pomo. I'm not flush just now, but I can let you have enough cash for tickets and maybe a little extra."

Beth nodded, relief a hard lump in her throat. The plan sounded logical, believable, authenticated by Miles' convincing enjoyment of the cleverness of his intrigue and of Eva's anticipated defeat. "About what time will it be? What time should I be ready to go?"

"I'm not sure exactly. Depends on how long it takes this friend of mine to set up the emergency. I told him to make it as early as possible, so you better start listening for Pete's truck anytime after nine."

"All right. I'll be ready."

He got up then, snubbed his cigarette and moved to the door. Opening it slightly, he stepped out into the hall, listening, and for a moment Beth hoped. But then he came back in and locked the door and the hope died. He was grinning whitely. "Now about my fee," he said. "A little reward for my time and trouble and hard-earned cash."

Although she had known it would happen, she had made no plans. No plans to fail or resolutions to be broken this time. There could be no defense except to accept that it would happen and her reaction would be whatever it would be, and then it would be over, and she and Paul would go away—and the leaving would be her defense and her victory.

When his hands were on her, she stepped away saying, "I'll do it," and, surprised, he said, "Good. Good, you do it," and she undressed quickly, watching him. Naked then, she still watched him, seeing the glazing stare of his eyes and the stretch of his threatening smile, as he bared his hard narrow body and reached out for her with white knuckled hands. Something, perhaps the watching, angered him so that he punished her with obscene words and, although she did not resist him, with brutal battering force, so that she was in real pain. But even then a part of her stood outside the violence and went on watching until at last his straining, grimacing face contorted into a shuddering, gasping ending. When he got up from her and stood looking down, she was still in pain and angry, but the anger, too, was different—urgently, insistently different. While he was dressing she got up slowly and stood against the wall, almost forgetting him in her effort to grasp and understand the difference and its importance. But then he looked up from stomping into his boots and suddenly his face twisted with fury, and he stepped close, grabbing her hair and bending her head far back and hitting her hard across the lips and cheek. She was terrified then, thinking he might kill her, but because there was no use trying to run or plead, she only stood still with her head up, crying. And then he went out the door without looking back, and she stood for a while longer before she realized that it was over. And then she put on clothing and went upstairs.

Later when she was in bed the strange anger grew stronger, a clean flame where before there had been only a corroding acid. And before she slept, there was the beginning of a cautious hope that life might someday be explainable in terms of realities that were no longer irretrievably beyond her grasp.

23

W H E N she woke, before daylight, the hopefulness
had been replaced by terror—of the day that was
dawning and its more than sufficient evils. There was,
she now realized, the definite possibility that Miles
would still be angry, so angry that he might change
his mind about helping. And even if he carried out his
plans, there were other terrors, other threats and
dangers. There was Eva and her keen probing eyes.
Had she been deceived? Had Beth's careful enactment
of normal dinnertime behavior fooled her the evening
before? But the greatest danger would come from—
would be when—they left the house, even if Eva and
Pete and Matthew were all busy with Miles at the
garages beyond the south wing, because there would
still be the House. She would still have to escape from
the surrounding walls. She switched on the light, and
the dark fantasies faded.

By seven o'clock she had packed a few necessities

and some articles of clothing in a picnic basket—everything else would have to be left behind. When she had finished, she stood by the window watching the patio as she waited for Paul to awaken. It had rained hard during the night, and the huge expanse of stone gleamed in the morning light like a gray sea. At half past seven the door of the greenhouse opened and Miles came out onto the patio. He stopped for a moment, looked around casually, and then glanced up at her window. In the sharp morning light she could see him clearly—the pale eyes, the harsh, tight-skinned face. Her fingers touched the painful shadow on her cheek and the anger flared strong and healthy, mingling with relief that so far, at least, he was doing what he had said he would do. Skirting the fountain, he crossed the patio and disappeared down the slope towards the corrals. She would get Paul up now, feed him his breakfast, and then, from the kitchen with the western window open, she would listen for the sound of Jasper's truck.

She wakened Paul gently, guiltily, because he didn't know they were going and would not be told the truth until they were safely in Pomo. She felt herself a traitor, but there was no other way. She could not have Paul resisting as she tried to get him out of the House, over the hill, and through the deserted town.

Paul awakened in a strange mood. Sitting on the edge of his cot, touseled and heavy-eyed, he suddenly stiffened, his eyes growing wide and watchful. He sat motionless, head cocked, listening, or sensing something out of the ordinary. "What's the matter?" he asked.

"Nothing's the matter," she told him, "except it's getting late and I've been planning for us to go on a long walk today. We'll need to get started soon."

He brightened. "Okay. Can I ride my hobby horse?" He slid off the bed and padded off for the bathroom. It was almost immediately afterwards that Beth heard the sound of the truck.

The wheezing grind was unmistakable—but it was much too early. Miles had said he would already be at the new barnyard when the call came, but it had only been a few minutes since he had gone down to get Tartar. Panicky, her mind blank with confusion, Beth ran down the hall to the old house. Crouching on the stairs where a part of the driveway was visible through the transom, she watched as an old blue truck labored into view. Pete Jasper climbed down from the driver's seat.

She ran again then—quick and quiet—stopping outside the bathroom door long enough to be sure Paul was still there—water splashing in the basin—back to the window.

The patio was empty, the gray stone still shining wetly. The greenhouse, its panes steamed and misted, glittered in the first reach of the morning sun. The door opened then, and Eva and Pete came out, Carl close behind them. Eva and Pete were talking, gesturing, and then Eva spoke to Carl and he ran, eager and clumsy, to the far edge of the patio terrace and shouted, waving his arms. After a moment he called again and gestured, a beckoning circle, and then trotted back to Eva and Pete near the greenhouse. A moment later Tartar surged up the hill and onto the patio.

Beth had turned to go—to rush Paul, half-dressed, breakfastless, out of the house and over the hill to the waiting place by the highway—but the iron hooves, ringing with threat, immobilized her like a siren's scream, and she turned back. The moment of choice had passed, and she stayed by the window, terrified by something as yet unseen, while the bronze horse paced forward. High and tight, like a coiled spring of tremendous power, Tartar crossed the gray stones, and Miles, erect, easy in the saddle, lifted one hand in a showy salute of greeting—parading his great bronze dragon before Pete and Carl—and Eva. He was past the fountain near the stone bench when Tartar shied, leaping sideways with dazing suddenness. And Miles, caught off guard, toppled, clutched and grabbed awkwardly to keep from falling. As Tartar retreated backwards, slipping and sliding, Carl laughed excitedly, clapping his hands. But then Miles regained his balance, pulled a quirt from his boot, and brought it down violently on the horse's head and neck.

Then Tartar seemed to go mad with fear or rage. Exploding into the air in a high twisted leap, he came down shatteringly, head low, stiff-legged, staggered on the wet stone, and leaped again. But Miles was prepared now and, incredibly, he rode the hurtling leaps and violent landings with ease, his teeth gleaming as he lashed out again and again with the heavy whip.

The leaps lengthened then and changed direction. Tartar crashed across the patio, and as Pete and Carl and Eva scattered for safety, Miles laughed out loud. Almost directly below Beth's window the horse leaped

209

again, twisting into a great bow, came down crookedly, and fell violently onto his front knees. But, miraculously, Miles kept his seat, and when Tartar staggered to his feet, the whip came down again across his head and ears. Squealing, Tartar reared high onto his hind legs, hooves lashing, and staggered backwards while the whip still rose and fell, until he was beyond balance, beyond stopping, and the greenhouse was behind him. And then they fell into an explosion of glittering light.

Light and sound erupted, fountained, and streamed down. Slashing, screaming daggers of light rained downward into a gaping vortex where red darkness heaved and thrashed. Something screamed once, inhumanly, and then Tartar erupted from the dark ruin and ran unevenly, lurching across the patio, the bronze hide smeared and streaming a thicker color that flowed into a trail of horror across the gray stone, to plunge from sight into the valley. In the dark ruin of the greenhouse something moved once, sluggishly, and then was still.

24

P A U L came running into the room, his eyes flat with fear. "What was that? What was that?" he cried. "What went crash, crash, crash?"

All Beth could think of was keeping him away from the window. Catching him, clutching him in her arms, she scurried, choking with horror, down the stairs into the kitchen. She put him down then, and when she could produce sound, she told him that it was only the greenhouse—that the greenhouse had broken and fallen down.

He stared at her, reading her horror. "No, no," he insisted. "What crashed? What crashed, Umm?"

"It was the greenhouse, really. It really was, Paul." Fighting the shriek in her lungs, she shut her mind to everything except the effort to control her voice, to keep a calm and steady tone.

But Paul still stared, his eyes blank and opaque. "I want to see it. I want to see the greenhouse."

"No, not now. We'll eat breakfast now, and then after awhile you can—see the greenhouse." When? How long? How long would it be before Miles was gone—before all trace of Miles was gone from the greenhouse?

If she had been capable of thinking clearly, if she had not been numb with shock and horror, she would have known enough to take Paul and leave then, immediately, under cover of the first confusion. But instead she thought only of calming herself and Paul by immersing them both in the performance of daily ritual. Forcing herself to deal with hot chocolate and oatmeal, she closed her mind to the reddening ruin of the greenhouse—until suddenly there was a new horror. The loud sharp report of a gun.

For moment she couldn't think what it meant, but then she knew, and it was not until then that she felt grief. Grief for Tartar who had been so fiercely beautiful, and whose rebellion had led to the terrible retreat across the gray stones, the fierce strength leaking a red trail down the hill to where they had found him, to end his pain and his rebellion. And then finally a strange angry grief for Miles. For Miles who had been a victim, too; a victim of his legacy of perverted power.

They stayed in the kitchen until Paul had eaten his breakfast, and by then it was too late. Paul was still at the table when there were footsteps in the hall, and Rachel came into the room. If Beth had not already been certain that Miles was dead, Rachel's pale frozen face would have told her.

"Eva wants to see you," Rachel said. "She's in the library."

"Eva?"

"Yes. She said to tell you she needs your help."

"And Paul?"

"I'll stay with Paul. I'll look after him until you get back."

"Gramma?" Instead of his usual enthusiastic rush of greeting, Paul came to Rachel slowly, his face anxious and questioning. Rachel knelt to greet him, and there was something in the bend and reach of her soft shapelessness that comforted Beth and made her willing to leave Paul, for the moment, in her care.

Eva was sitting at the library table, leaning slightly forward, both arms extended full length before her, her head held stiffly up and back. At the sound of the door she started, and when she saw Beth, she got quickly to her feet. Her face was blank and still. As Beth approached she held out both her hands. "Beth," she said. Her voice was steady, the dark, devouring eyes tearless.

"Miles?" Beth asked.

Eva shook her head.

"I—I'm sorry."

"Yes. It's terrible. A terrible thing. An awful blow. Pete has gone to notify the authorities. These next few days will be very hard. Will you help us, my dear? There is something you can do that would be very helpful."

"What—what is it?"

"Come." Maintaining her hold on Beth's right hand, Eva moved to the door and out into the hall, leading Beth as one would a child. And Beth followed, her mind a frightened, directionless turmoil. What did Eva want of her? Where were they going?

Were they going—to Miles? Did Eva know what Miles had been planning to do and, perhaps blame her, Beth, for everything that had happened? Was she going to make her look at him—see what she had done? Beth hung back, trying to free her hand from Eva's grasp, but the grip only tightened, and Eva moved on up the central stairway and down the second floor hall. As they rounded the corner Beth saw Matthew. Arms folded, he was leaning against the wall next to a door—the closet door that led to the unfinished wing. The door was open.

Plunging backward, Beth pried at Eva's fingers but the hand was like steel, and then Matthew was on her other side, and between them, she was being forced forward, into the closet, up the short flight and down the echoing skeletal upper hall of the unfinished wing.

She struggled frantically, her feet sliding, scraping over the rough wood, kicking up heavy clouds of dust. "Where are you taking me?" she gasped. "What are you going to do?"

"We're not going to hurt you." Eva's voice was strained and disjointed by the force of the struggle. "Unless you force us to. It's just that we feel that we must—make other arrangements for you—temporarily. Just until the confusion of the next few days is over. We're sorry this is necessary—but we just don't feel that you're to be trusted—for the next few days. There'll be strangers—people coming and going."

When the struggle ended, when her arms were at last released, they were in the parlor, in Calvin's parlor.

"Let her go," Eva said. "Go watch the door." And

then there was only Eva holding her, and then she, too, stepped away. Beth ran towards the door, but Matthew was there, holding it, and then Eva was beside him.

"You're not going to leave me here—alone—in this room?" Beth begged, pleaded, knowing that they would, that they meant to, unless she could make them understand, make them see—"I'll die, I'll die, if you leave me here it will kill me."

She was clutching at Eva, and Eva caught her wrists, fending her off. Even then, clutching against Beth's frenzied struggling, Eva's voice was calm, soothing. "It will only be for a short time. A few days should be all that's necessary. And Rachel and Matthew have done everything they could to be sure that you'll be comfortable. There's water on the table, a comfortable bed. . . ."

Beth was sobbing, choking. "Paul," she gasped. "What about Paul?"

Eva shook her head reprovingly. "Surely you're not afraid that we won't be able to look after Paul for a few days. We'll take very good care of him, I promise you. He'll lack for absolutely nothing."

Eva smiled and it was the smile, the unshakable serenity in the face of death and dungeons and a child stolen from its mother that drove Beth over the edge into abject terror. "No! No!" she screamed. "Don't shut me up here. Don't take Paul away from me. I won't try to take him away. I won't talk to anyone. Just let me out. Please, please let me out." She lunged towards the door, but Matthew caught and held her while Eva went out quickly, and then he shoved her hard so that she staggered, fell backwards; and when

215

she reached the door again, it was closed and locked.

Fists pounding, beating on the door, screaming, the scream blurring to a wordless shriek on and on higher and higher until nothing else was left but scream, endless and uncontrollable.

25

S H E lay huddled in the dust, her arms around her head. There was pain—throat swollen, scalded with screams, legs cramped beneath her. Very slowly, slyly, she raised her head. Dim light, one small bulb high up, beneath it the two tables, but no tools now. Other things—buckets, basins, towels. Against the wall a chamber pot and a bed with blankets.

She raised her head a little farther and searched the corners of the room, moving only her eyes so he wouldn't see that she was looking. There were shadows in the corners, darkest in the far end, beyond the fireplace. Too dark to see him there. She watched and waited for a long time until the pain in her legs grew stronger and the cold ached in her back and fingers. When the cold and pain balanced against the terror of the dark corner, she began to move. Very slowly she dragged herself to her feet, gripping the paneling, the doorknob. And then inching, creeping, her heart exploding, she crept against the wall, keeping her eyes on the dark place. At the bed, still watching, she pulled down the blankets and slowly, still watching, she climbed under—and snatched the covers over her head. King's X.

She lay in warm woolen darkness, curled in a tight ball. Under the cover is King's X, you can't catch me, my fingers are crossed, aly-aly-ox-in-free, now I lay me down to sleep, hiding, hiding, and no one knows where. There was a long gentle sinking, the darkness deepening, emptying, the only movement a slow drift of dim shadows. Old shadows, old safe rooms where the beautiful mermaid laughed and Miss Muffet sat at the table reading, swinging her legs, legs swinging—and running. She closed her eyes tighter, closed her mind to everything but the sinking darkness; but the running came back, white legs flashing in the darkness. Legs flashing, running, Willie Winkie running, running, stumbling, something tangled around her legs and something in her arms was getting heavier and heavier as she ran. Something in her arms that was—no, not Paul, I didn't decide, I don't know what I'm doing, not Paul.

But the running went on, she had remembered it now and it wouldn't go away and leave her alone in her hiding place. And because she had remembered there was no King's X anymore, no hiding place. She had remembered about Andy and she knew now that the chickens had been King's X; and Jonathan although he hadn't meant or wanted to had been King's X; and then Covenant Farm and Eva and Miles had all been King's X—until she remembered. But now

218

there was no King's X anymore, no Miss Muffet. There was only Beth—and Paul.

What were they doing to Paul? What would they teach him? How would they tempt him to become what they wanted him to be? He was so little, so helpless. How could he ever escape them. She had to help him somehow. It was all up to her.

After a while she sat up and looked at where she couldn't see anything in the corner darkness, to where he sucked up the darkness and held it around him so she would know that he was there. Terror flared, moaned in her throat, and then grew, not less, but familiar, an old wound. I know why she put me here, she told him. It's not just that it's far away and the windows are boarded to shut in the screaming. It's not just that. It's because you're here. Because she knows that I know you're here and that I'll die of fear of you, or else go into a hiding place forever. Like Rachel—Rachel in her soft, shapeless hiding place, and Matthew, too, behind his keyhole. I got this room like Matthew got the logging truck and Miles the falling daggers and Rachel—whatever awful thing Rachel got to make her go blurred and shapeless. I got this room so she could get Paul for you, and turn him into something evil so that the Farm can go on, and you can go on hiding here from whatever it is that's waiting for you. You see, she told him, I know all about it.

She stopped talking then and just sat on the bed trying to think clearly. There seemed to be something wrong with her head that kept her thoughts from running in a straight line from one thing to the next thing that ought to follow. As if something, the screaming maybe, had burned up all the little delicate connections in her mind so that there were only spaces left. She tried to force them, to will the connections back together, but it was no use. They had to grow, to heal quickly, so she would be able to understand and reason and decide. She had to be able to decide what it was in the dark corner that frightened her so—and if there was anything she could do to help Paul. After a while she began to feel a teeth-clenching spasm thing that turned out to be anger. I won't let them, she thought. I won't. At least not so easy. I don't see what I can do yet, but as soon as my mind gets better, I'll think of something, and I won't hide anymore.

A long time later there was a sound in the hall, and Matthew opened the door and held it for Rachel. Then he went back out, and Rachel came slumping and shuffling across the room to one of the tables, carrying a tray. She put the tray on the table, and then she took two folding chairs off the other table and set them up, one in front of the tray and the other one a little to one side. Then, without looking at Beth, she sat down in the farthest chair, folded her hands in her lap and stared at them. Beth went on sitting on the bed watching Rachel and beyond Rachel's bowed head, the dark, silent corner.

After a few minutes Rachel moved uneasily, her head twitching towards Beth. In her lap her hands were gripping each other. "I brought you your dinner," she said, low and mumbling. "I have to stay while you eat it."

Beth got up then from the bed and moved, limp

and dizzy, as if after a long illness, to the chair by the table. There was a napkin on the tray and under the napkin was stew in a bowl, bread and butter, a pot of tea, an apple and a piece of raisin cake. At the sight of the food her throat contracted, painfully.

"I don't think I could eat anything—yet," she said. "Could you just leave it here, for later?"

Rachel's eyes came up slowly. The huge irises looked faded. "I can't leave it. She said I was to wait until you had finished. I have to take the dishes—and things—back with me."

Beth nodded. She understood, she would not be allowed knives or broken glass. She stared at the stew wondering if she could swallow.

"Try to eat a little." Rachel was whispering and Beth wondered if it was Matthew outside the door, or the thing in the corner, that might hear. "I won't be able to come back until tomorrow."

She ought to eat—stay strong—so it wouldn't be so easy. . . . She scooped up a spoonful of the stew, but her throat tightened. She shook her head. "My throat is swollen," she told Rachel, "from screaming."

Something contracted, flinched, in Rachel's face. One hand came up, reached, and dropped again. "Don't worry—try not to worry about Paul," she said. "I'll watch him. I'll try to watch him all I can."

Without warning tears erupted. Beth fell on her knees in front of Rachel, clutching her hands. "Please, please Rachel," she sobbed. "Help us. Help me get away, for Paul's sake. I know you love him. Won't you help us to get away?"

Rachel struggled to her feet, pulling her hands roughly out of Beth's grasp. Her face had gone white

221

and stiff. "No, no. I can't. I can't help you." Clumsy, frantic, she spread the napkin on the table, put the bread and apple and cake on it, and scurried away with the rest. Matthew opened the door again, locked it, and their footsteps went up the stairs and away.

Time seemed to have stopped moving. For an unnamable amount of time her mind wandered, drifted, and when she tried to force it to plan or reason, scattered into panic. She clung to the bed as if to sanctuary, leaving it only to use the chamber pot, creeping to it with heart pounding, eyes stretched with watching, as if to move nearer was to tempt the thing in the corner. But it still waited, letting her finish and scurry back to the bed, gasping with fright. At last she fell asleep and dreamed so vividly that her dreams blended into waking fantasy and continued when she slept again.

She dreamed the Farmhouse, with towering rooms and endless hallways. She dreamed a young Margaret on the stairway, dressed in white and spangled by crystal light, her eyes a dazzling extravagance of beauty. She dreamed the greenhouse, its glittering walls surrounding a lush green jungle where the damp air stirred with swelling and budding and two children bent their dark, vivid heads over a strange flower and watched as it grew larger and larger, pulsing with life, spreading out around them until they were surrounded by its bright unnatural glory. She dreamed the dining room with many people around the table. Margaret, again, not the shining girl on the staircase, but still young and lovely—the sleek chiseled beauty of a young Eva—Matthew, slimmer, smooth-skinned, but already weak and twisted. Lucien, she knew by his dark beauty—and next to him a soft brown girl, slender and supple, whose haunted eyes were Rachel's. And there were children, too, a glowing child who was Jonathan, a sharp, pale Miles, and Carl, a small, dull echo of Jonathan. And at the head of the table there was darkness, the thick gathered darkness of the corner beyond the firepace. Beth woke, stared into that darkness, and slept to dream again.

Wide awake at last, she remembered that Rachel had promised to come again the next day. Time had obviously gone crazy, but surely much more than a day had passed since then. Perhaps Eva had not let her come. Perhaps Eva knew that Beth had stopped hiding, and had decided to let her die in other ways— to starve. With that thought there came hunger that quickly grew strong enough to force her out of bed and across the long reach of floor to the table. Snatching up the napkin, she scurried back to sit on the bed, back against the wall, eyes on the darkness, while she ate ravenously.

Later, as if the food had contained a small dose cf courage, she left the bed again and went to a window. There was no glass and the planks that covered the opening were massive, close-set and heavily nailed. She fingered a crack between two planks but they were either double or overlapped so that no light penetrated, or else it was dark everywhere. She turned quickly. The darkness behind the fireplace was deep and quiet. She waited, stood her ground, until the thunder in her chest lessened, and then she crept on past the corner to the door. She ran her hands over the heavy wood and large old-fashioned lock. A sudden surge of anger made her shake the door, but with the thick thudding rattle, terror struck, like a cold hand at the base of her spine, and she scuttled in mindless panic back to the bed. It was sometime later that Rachel came again.

Rachel brought breakfast, and this time Beth ate slowly and talked very carefully to Rachel who sat again half-turned away, staring at her clenching hands. Beth did not ask Rachel to help or even about Paul, although her throat ached with the effort to hold back his name. Instead, she talked of Jonathan, of a long-ago Jonathan who had been Rachel's Paul. At first Rachel's answers were brief and hesitant, but then, as Beth kept her voice calm and even, Rachel relaxed enough to let her mind go back. Yes, Jonathan had loved apples then too, just as he had as an adult; and music and maps of distant places, and animals of all kinds, and flowers. . . .

"He told me once," Beth said, "that you taught him the names of the flowers."

"He told you that . . ." Rachel's eyes were like wounds. She hid them quickly, looking again at her hands. When she spoke again, her voice had faded. "Yes, Jonathan loved flowers and animals almost as much as . . ." She stopped then and looked up too quickly, before Beth had time to hide the pain. Rachel's hand came up again in a gesture like a hopeless blessing, and then, gathering up the dishes with trembling hands, her face blind and blank, she hurried away.

It was some time after that, that for the first time there began to be an idea, a plan. It was not until then that Beth's mind had begun to seem capable of considering possibilities, evaluating them and moving on to decisions. It was clear that there was no way to force her way out of her prison. And even if she did somehow manage it, there would still be Eva, and the others who would be sent after her—Matthew and Carl or the Jaspers. There was no way to break out. Her plan was less than that—less courageous, less of everything, only a beginning. She would ask Rachel to tell Eva that she wanted to talk to her. And when Eva came she would pretend to be broken, to have gone into hiding like Rachel and Matthew. She would say that she hadn't meant to run away with Paul, would never even think of it. She would pretend that she had given up forever, and if she did it well enough, maybe Eva would let her out—let her out where she could, at least, see Paul and be near him.

When Rachel came again, Matthew came in, too, carrying another chamber pot. As he lurched across the room, his eyes rolled like marbles to look at Beth sitting on the bed, her back against the wall. He exchanged the pots and went out, and she waited until he had gone before she said anything. The rolling eyes had made her angry, and she wanted to say something about Matthew's chore, about the things that he and others had done and would do because Eva told them to. But she knew better. She knew now that she must not talk about anything that would frighten Rachel away. So she talked again about Jonathan and the distant past, asking harmless questions and eating very slowly to keep Rachel with her as long as possible. When there was nothing more to eat and Beth was about to ask to see Eva, Rachel suddenly reached into her pocket.

"Here," she said, thrusting something into Beth's hand. "Don't let Matthew see it. She didn't say I could bring them to you."

Beth glanced into her hand. It was her toothbrush, lipstick, comb, things that didn't matter—only they did. She threw her arms around Rachel's neck and kissed the sagging cheek. "Thank you. Oh, thank you, Rachel." The tears were not for the lipstick, but for Rachel helping, wanting to help.

But the lipstick ruined the plan. All the things that Rachel had brought were Beth's own, things that she had packed in the picnic basket to take with them when they ran away. She had forgotten all about the basket. But if Eva had it now, she knew what Beth had been planning, and she would never let her out, never let her be with Paul.

After that she was, more than ever, haunted, tormented, obsessed with fear for Paul. She slept very little. Sitting on the bed she stared into the dim circle of light that held the darkness back beyond the fireplace, and saw, not the darkness, but Paul. Her own Paul as he had been, the soft, blunt face framed by clumps of curls, the wide eyes that saw dreams so clearly, the solemn smile. What had they done to him? How would they bend him to fit their evil legend? With what would they tempt him? The dark thing in the corner had wanted power and beauty and had given death. Lucien perhaps had wanted less and had not killed; but his beauty had been another added power, and he had had his victims among the living. Whatever had been offered Jonathan, and had been asked of him, had made him run away from

226

Covenant Farm and perhaps from life. And now they had Paul. When she slept at last, she dreamed of Paul, and Rachel came with breakfast while she was still sleeping.

She woke slowly, drugged with sleep, but alert enough to remember that she must ask Rachel about the basket—but not immediately, in case the question frightened her away. Staggering to the table, Beth splashed her face with cold water from the bucket and dried it hard, scrubbing away the stupor of the stunned sleep that comes finally after hours of insomnia. She saw then that there was a difference in Rachel.

There was a tension, a firmness, in the slack blur of Rachel's face, and a light in the wide-set eyes that might almost be excitement. She answered Beth's questions, the harmless casual ones that had to come first, with an air of preoccupation.

"What day is it?" Beth asked, and for a moment she seemed not to hear.

"Day?" she said then. "Oh, what day? The—ninth. Yes, it's the ninth."

Only two days. It seemed impossible that she had been there only two days. It had been a lifetime. She had died and been reborn and then had lived a long painful lifetime.

She considered asking about Miles—if there had been a funeral—if there would be one. And she fought against asking about Paul—if he was all right—if he asked about her. Instead she asked about the weather, because Rachel must not be frightened before she found out about the basket. But then, when she had almost finished eating, Rachel got up suddenly and came to bend very close. Her whisper trembled.

"I brought something—something of yours. I found them in the trash." Reaching inside the loose neck of her baggy dress, she brought out a small package tied in cloth and put it into Beth's lap. "No, don't open it now. Not until I've gone. And when I come back this evening, I'll take them away again." She leaned closer. "They mustn't know."

Beth nodded and tucked the package inside her sweater. Rachel was gathering up the dishes. "Rachel. About the lipstick, the things you brought me yesterday—where did you get them?"

"From the basket. The things you had packed in the basket."

"Does Eva know? About the basket?"

"Yes. She sent me to your room to get Paul's things. I found the basket; but before I could unpack it, she came in. She saw the basket."

Then there was no hope. No hope that she could get Eva to set her free. Rachel put her hand on Beth's shoulder. She spoke as if to a child in pain. "Don't. Don't cry. It didn't matter. She knew anyway. She knew before that you were planning to run away. She told me so."

How could she have known? She had known that Beth wanted to go, but not that she had planned to run away. How could she have known? Unless Miles . . . "Did she know about Miles, too?"

"About Miles?"

"Yes, that he was going to help us get away. Or at least he told me that he . . ." She stopped, staring

228

at Rachel. The dark eyes were rimmed in white, the face congealed into a doughy lump of terror. "Rachel. What is it?" She clutched Rachel's arm, slowing her retreat.

"Don't you see?" Rachel hissed, jerking herself free. "Don't you understand why—what happened to Miles. . . ." A humped, shapeless retreat, feet scuffling, dishes shuddering on the tray, and Rachel was gone.

Beth sat against the wall, staring at the dark place. Was that really why Miles had died—why Tartar had fallen—why the daggers had streamed down into the reddening darkness? How could it have been? How could it have been, she asked the darkness, and then remembered. Remembered how Tartar had dodged away near the place that Margaret watched from her window—the place that the poor red dog watched, trembling. It was a long hour later that Beth remembered the package that Rachel had left.

The first time she read the letters, she cried with joy. With the joy of knowing that Warren had not forgotten—that someone somewhere outside the Farmhouse thought about her, that a world still existed outside her prison.

Four of the letters in the package were her own—letters that she had written to Warren and that Eva had taken with her to mail on her way to the new barnyard. The others were all from Warren to Beth. The oldest ones, written several weeks ago, were funny and chatty, but the later ones were worried, angry. The latest one was dated October 3, only six days ago. In the last letter Warren had written, "A few weeks ago, after I had gotten really upset about not hearing from you, I wrote to a friend of a friend, who works for a firm in Eureka, and asked if he would do a little research for me—see what he could find out about the Coreys. I got the answer just yesterday. There's nothing too definite, but enough to make me think that it's possible that you've gotten yourself into some kind of weird situation. So, being by nature a nosy officious type, I think I'll just take it on myself to drop in and see if you're not writing because you're just too busy and happy, or some other less salubrious reason. I'm coming up that way, anyway, on business, at least as far as San Francisco. I'm not due there until the fifteenth, so there's still time to head me off if you really want to. But unless I hear from you, and soon, with some really convincing reasons why you don't want, or need, to see me, I'll be arriving at the Corey's ancestral plantation on or about the seventeenth of the month."

The seventeenth was still eight days away—an eternity. So much—far too much—could happen in eight days. Eva could have typed a letter, pretending to be Beth, telling him not to come. And even if he came, they could tell him she'd gone away, on a visit, or for good. There would be no way he could prove differently—nothing he could do. The letters had been opened when Beth got them—opened and, no doubt, read, so Eva would be prepared, would know what to do to get rid of Warren. So nothing was greatly changed by the letters, but still Beth cried over them and sat all day holding them in her hands.

Rachel came back that night, still stiff and cold with fear. She said almost nothing, refused to answer even the most harmless questions, and when she left

230

she insisted on taking Warren's letters with her. Beth almost cried again to see them go.

Beth dreamed about Paul again that night. Terrible dreams about Paul in danger, walking on a cliff's edge, trapped in a burning house, and skipping down a road following a vague hooded figure that stopped and beckoned and went on, and Paul followed, skipping, not seeing the greedy, empty eyes under the hood of darkness.

All the next day and the next Rachel refused to talk, and on the third day Beth could see that she had been crying. Fear for Paul, terrible despairing fear, made Beth unable to eat. At last she turned to Rachel and took her by both arms, shaking her. "You have to tell me. What are they doing to Paul? What is it? You've got to tell me."

Rachel turned her head away, averting her eyes. "I don't know," she said. "I haven't seen him much lately. Eva keeps him with her. I don't know."

"But what have you been crying about? Why are you crying?"

Rachel stared at her. "Not about Paul," she said. "About Jonathan. Don't you remember what day this is?"

"Day? What day this is?"

"Yes. Today is the twelfth. The twelfth of October."

Beth shook her head.

"The day Jonathan died. The day of the accident."

"No. Not October. Jon died in August. The twenty-first of August."

"August—August—are you sure?"

"How could I not be sure?" Beth asked.

231

Rachel was on her feet now. Her face looked stunned, flattened, as if by a blow. "The twenty-first of August?" she whispered. "Summer before last?"

"Yes," Beth said, "in August, the last of August." Rachel turned and walked away, shuffling, stood with her back to Beth and began to make soft whining noises deep in her throat, noises like an animal in pain. Then she writhed, clutching her hair and fell on her knees, and the whine grew louder, shriller, until it became a shriek.

"Rachel, don't, don't. What is it? What's the matter." Beth was kneeling, trying to lift the huddled body, take it into her arms. And then someone was pulling at her, lifting her away from Rachel. It was Matthew, pulling Rachel to her feet, half leading and half carrying her to the door. The door slammed, and Beth scuttled across the room to huddle on the bed.

She was still there, still huddled, when she heard the door open again, and heavy dragging footsteps. She raised her head to see Matthew at the table, gathering the dishes, eyes darting towards Beth on the bed.

"Rachel? How—how is she?"

Matthew grinned. "She's all right. Just hysterical. Always has been. What happened in here? You do something to upset her?"

"No, no. I don't know."

"Well, she'll get over it. She has before."

26

T H E Y were standing over her when she awoke, Matthew and Eva. Loops of heavy rope dangled from Matthew's hands and his eyes jiggled with excitement, but Eva's eyes were serene and certain. She reached down and took Beth's wrists in strong hands and held them while Beth fought and pleaded, and Matthew tied her feet with the heavy rope. Then they put her hands behind her back and tied them there, but she went on pleading, promising not to run away, until they forced a cloth between her teeth and then taped her mouth, strapping tape again and again across her face. When she couldn't move or speak, they stood looking down at her for a moment, Matthew twitching and gasping and Eva smiling.

"I'm sorry," Eva said kindly. "It's too bad. But it's the only way." She reached down and pulled up the covers tucking them in gently around Beth's chin, and then went away.

There was no escape, no King's X hiding place. Only the certain knowledge that it was coming, the horror that her dreams had threatened. She had tried, had struggled, but not until it was too late. When there still might have been time, she had not struggled. She had given herself and Paul to them, to Eva, to Miles and to the darkness that watched and waited in corners and hallways in the shadow of the sycamore and under pyramids of deadly glass. Its time of waiting was almost over. The door was opening.

The door was opening and Paul was coming in. Paul coming in all alone, looking back as the door closed behind him and then down at the thing in his hand. The thing a gun, oh my God, a gun in Paul's hand! Paul standing tiny and alone in the huge room, looking around and then seeing her and coming closer. Coming toward the bed slowly, his eyes huge, dark in his pale face, dear loved face and tawny hair and eyes wide and dark. Dark eyes blank, stunned-looking, oh Paul what have they done to you? Close now beside the bed looking down at her taped face and crying eyes. "Umm?" Yes, yes, nodding, saying yes, yes, Paul it's Umm, but only making noises strangled smothered noises. "Umm?" His chin trembling. "Did you run away and leave me, Umm? Eva says you ran away. Did you, Umm?" Shaking her head, making the awful noises. Paul reaching out, touching her face, wiping at the tears with a cold little hand and picking for a moment at the tape, but with only his left hand because the other still held the gun. "Eva says you ran away. Eva gave me this gun and showed me how. Eva says I can have the pony tomorrow. Tomorrow, really, Umm." Looking at her expectantly, as if for approval. No, no, Paul, don't, oh God, don't let this happen.

Paul staring at her long, hard, and then down at the gun and then, "Is this a really gun, Umm? Will it hurt? Is it a really gun?" Nodding frantically, crying choking. And then Paul put down the gun very carefully on the floor and climbed up on the bed beside her, his arms around her neck and his cheek against hers. Oh God, thank you, thank you, thank you.

After a little while Paul sat up and wiped her tears with his hands and then with the covers and began to pick again at the tape across her mouth until finally an edge loosened and it came off.

"Oh, Paul, darling. I'm so glad you're here, so glad to see you. Darling, I didn't run away. I never would have run away and left you. I've just been shut up here in this room all the time. Eva shut me up here and wouldn't let me out. Eva was lying to you, telling you things that weren't true."

He looked at her solemnly. "I thought," he said. "I thought maybe." His face was thoughtful, sad. "There wasn't any pony?" he asked. "There wasn't really any pony?"

"No, Paul. Not really."

He nodded, sighing. "Come on, Umm, let's go. I don't like it here."

"I can't, Paul. I'm tied up. Eva and Matthew tied me up. Pull down the covers and see if you can untie me. Maybe you can untie the knots."

He couldn't. The heavy ropes had been tightly knotted, and even though Paul tried until he was whimpering with frustration, the ropes held firm. She told him to stop then, and sent him instead to the table for water. Her throat ached, burned from the smothered crying.

Paul climbed on a chair and was dipping water from the bucket when he stopped and stood still facing the dark corner. "Paul, Paul. Come here. Come back here to me. Never mind about the water. Come here."

But the cup was full, and he got down slowly from the chair, slopping a little, and looked back once towards the corner, before he came, slowly, holding the cup in both hands, walking very carefully. She raised her head as far as she could, and he held the cup, tipping it too much so that some of the water ran down her chin. Over his shoulder she could see the gathered darkness. Paul turned too, following her eyes.

"Paul," she whispered. "What is it? Can you see— someone?"

But he only looked for so long without answering that she wondered if he had heard, before he nodded slowly. "Yes," he said. "Someone." He turned back then, and she tried to hide her fright, but not quickly enough. He stared, his forehead puckered with worry.

"But it's not really, Umm. Not really."

"What do you mean, not really? What's not really?"

"He isn't. When you don't look at him, he isn't." He put the cup down carefully on the floor next to the gun and climbed back up on the bed and lay down beside her, one arm around her neck.

27

THERE was a sound outside the door, a faint whisper of movement.

"Paul," Beth whispered. "Someone's out there. Outside the door. Is it . . . ?"

"Eva, maybe. Maybe it's still Eva."

Oh God, of course it would be Eva. Waiting outside the door to come in and—no, not to do it herself. If it had just been Beth's life she was after, there would have been easier ways. But waiting to come in to be sure that it was done. To use all her strength against Paul's innocence, to force him to go through with the terrible bargain she had prepared for him. It was Eva waiting, and nothing could be done.

But then, suddenly, there was another sound. Loud, heavy footsteps in the upper hall, coming nearer, and then someone calling. A thick, slurred voice shouting something unintelligible. And the soft movement again near the door, and then sharp quick footsteps diminishing, retreating up the stairs.

"Carl," Paul said. "Carl called Eva? Was it, Umm?"

"Yes, I think so. Paul, we have to get out of here. We have to try the ropes again. The ropes, Paul—Paul, what is it?"

He had turned quickly, blocking off her view of the door. Before she could maneuver, twist, and lift to where she could see around him, he said, "Gramma?" It was a question, uncertain, tentative, and then Beth saw why.

For a moment she wasn't sure either. The quick, alert turn and the darting eyes were not Rachel. With the soft shamble gone, the dusky skin paled and blotched, the long hair hanging in tangled strands, she seemed a stranger. Under a faded flannel gown her tensely erect body seemed slimmer, younger, and she moved light and quick on bare feet. Against the soft dullness of the flannel there was a sharp streak of light. A knife.

"Gramma," Paul slid from the bed and ran.

Fear surged. "Paul, no. Come back. Rachel, don't—"

But Paul's arms were around Rachel's waist and she was bending over him, the knife gleaming against the bright plaid of his shirt. She was hugging, patting, the knife flashing, and Beth's mind rocked with crazy fear. But the knife was not for Paul, and he skipped beside Rachel as she came on across the room towards the bed

"Rachel. Rachel, I—"

"It's all right. I came to tell you something. There's something you have to know."

"The knife?"

238

She looked down then, and for a moment seemed surprised to see it there. "From the kitchen," she said. "I was going to make her let me in to tell you. Yes," she nodded sharply, her eyes glinting with fear or determination. "I was going to. She left Carl to watch me, but I tricked him and got away and came here, but I looked down, from the hall, and saw her here by the door. So I went back to the kitchen and got the knife. I was going to make her let me in." Rachel stared at the knife with a kind of crazy desperate pride. "I was going to, but I heard Carl coming so I hid and Carl called her and she went with him. But I was going to make her let me in. . . ."

"Rachel, we have to get away quickly before they come back. Could you cut the ropes. Please, Rachel. Please help us."

"Yes, yes. I'll help." Beth rolled, flopped, face to the wall, and felt the blade between her wrists, sawing at the rope. "I helped Jonathan when he left, and they made me sorry. But that doesn't matter. Not anymore. Paul must go away. You must take Paul— Paul. . . ."

The sawing stopped, the blade hanging slack between Beth's wrists. She twisted to see Rachel holding Paul's face between her hands. "Take him away. Far away. Live in a city, put him in school with other children. He'll forget, be all right, he'll be all right, ordinary, like other children."

"Rachel, please. The rope. We have to hurry. They'll come back."

"Yes, yes." The sawing went on, and stopped again. "I came—I came to tell you—something." The pale face blank staring and then remembering. "I came to tell you what they did. You must know what they did. They were there, all of them, Eva and Miles and Matthew. They said they were going to see Jonathan, to ask him to come back to see Lucien before he died. But when they came back, they told me he wouldn't come. They said he was all right, married, happy, but that he wouldn't come back even for a day. And then on the twelfth of October they told me there had been an accident and that he was dead. They said Jonathan died on the twelfth of October. But they were there in Los Angeles in August. On the twenty-first of August, they were all there."

There was time then only to hear what Rachel said—not to think or feel it. "Rachel, the ropes, please hurry."

Her wrists were free then. She rubbed at the pain, rolling on her back. "My feet now, Rachel. Please hurry." But moving to the foot of the bed, Rachel's foot touched the gun and she stopped and picked it up, turning it slowly in her hands.

"It's Eva's," she said. "How—"

"Eva gave it to me, Gramma. Eva told me I could have the pony tomorrow. Eva showed me how to shoot it, but I didn't because it's a really gun. Did you know that, Gramma?"

Rachel stared at Paul and then her face twisted, as if in pain. She seemed to stiffen, her head jerking to one side, her arms extending in front of her with the gun still clasped in both hands. The soft whining noise was beginning again, and as it got louder, her face went blind and blank. She turned away and moved stiffly, robotlike towards the door. Beth called after her, begged her to come back, but she went on

240

out the door and up the stairs. Alone again with Paul but now with her hands free, Beth cut the rope on her ankles, stood painfully, stumbled, limped and ran, dragging Paul beside her. Fear ran with her, choking and tripping—promised ambush at every corner—followed after, threatening pursuit. But the closet door hung open and the hall was empty, and the stairs. Part way down, Paul stumbled, unable to keep up, and she snatched him up and ran with him, ran dangerously, and near the bottom fell, hurting them both. But she scrambled up and ran again, Paul crying now but running fast, his feet flying, skimming the ground. They were halfway down the hill when they heard the first shot, and soon afterwards another, and then more. The gate was locked, but she lifted Paul over the fence, climbed it, and went on running beside the road. A car came—faces stared as she screamed and waved—and went on by. Then a truck came and stopped.

"Good God, lady. You want to get killed? Get the hell out of the road." But he listened, and then helped them into the cab. Paul cried softly all the way to Sturmville, but Beth was suddenly numbly calm. It was later, when they told her what she already knew—that Rachel had shot Eva and Matthew and then herself—that she became hysterical.

28

S H E came out of the bedroom to the window that overlooked the kiddie yard. Paul was still in the sandbox with the chubby blond boy with no front teeth. Gary, if she remembered correctly. Paul was sticking twigs into a mound of sand, talking to Gary or to himself. He seemed all right now, but he had had nightmares again last night, moaning and crying in his sleep. She went back slowly to the bedroom to finish dressing.

Sitting on the edge of the bed, she began to pull on her panty hose, stopped to inspect a snag—and went on sitting, staring sightlessly at the loose thread. Last night when Paul had been moaning and whimpering in his sleep, she had stood beside his bed watching his moving lips, his head turning on the pillow. Dr. Werner had said that the dreams were a good thing, a necessary release. But then Dr. Werner tended towards a pragmatic optimism that sometimes seemed a little too predictable to be entirely convincing. Not that she always disagreed with him. There was for instance his theory about Paul's apparent lack of trauma about the gun. If Eva had accomplished what she had set out to do—if Paul had really meant to kill his mother for a pony—there would be some residue, some sign of uneasiness or guilt. And there seemed to be none at all. From the first he had spoken of the gun and the pony and of Eva's careful instructions as readily as he spoke of Mundy or the fuzzy bear that had recently taken up residence in his closet. Given such an adjustable reality, it was possible that Paul had made no clear distinction between a fictitious pony and a real gun, between Eva's pretenses and her horribly real intentions. Perhaps, in Eva's presence, confused and overwhelmed by her monstrous authority, he had seemed to play her insane game—but only played it, immunized by innocence from its terrible reality. Until Beth's reality intruded, and the game was over. Seen in this way, there did seem to be reason to hope that Paul's exposure to Eva's insanity had left no serious scars.

There were, however, things that Paul would not talk about. But Dr. Werner seemed inclined to minimize the importance of other exposures and the scars they might have inflicted. But when Paul cried out in his sleep or stood for long periods entranced, listening, she wasn't sure.

And as for her own scars? She was well aware that even now, six weeks and six hundred miles from Covenant Farm, there were still shadows that resisted the clear light of Dr. Werner's analysis—memories that would not be neatly labeled. Dr. Werner had

243

been cheerfully tolerant and understanding. It was, he said, thoroughly understandable, under the circumstances almost natural. She had been through a series of shattering experiences—had relived a long-suppressed trauma, and had been subjected to physical and emotional violation. It would have been almost unnatural if she had not been disoriented, subject to hysteria and hallucination. But there was scarcely any doubt that, in time, she would be able to see that everything that had happened could be rationally and realistically explained. But she wasn't sure.

There were times when she wasn't sure she hadn't been seeing clearly in Calvin's parlor. Times when she felt that what she had seen there had been almost her first glimpse of reality. As if she had seen there, for the first time, the real faces of terror, of evil, and of love. And then when it was over and the terror had had time to scream itself away, she had climbed up from exhaustion into a different world, fluid and unpredictable, frightening and exciting. She knew for certain that something—the knowledge that she had not killed Andy or driven Jon to suicide, or simply that she had faced the darkness and lived through it—had made her look at things quite differently.

Sighing, she got up, hobbled across the room, dabbed fingernail polish on the incipient run, and finished dressing. Then she went back to the window above the sandbox. She was still there when the doorbell rang.

In the last six weeks Warren had been—Warren. A good friend—a friend in her direst need, those first few days in Sturmville—a clever lawyer, a patiently insistent suitor, and most recently—very recently—a reinstated lover. As she opened the door, he proffered a box of animal cookies for Paul, a single rosebud, and a sheepish grin.

"Embarrassing," he said as Beth took the rosebud. "Maudlin actually, and hardly original. But on the way over here it occurred to me that under the circumstances—"

"Don't gloat," she said and held up her face to be kissed. He kissed her enthusiastically and then held her off to look.

"God. You're looking great today." He pulled her back against him. "And feeling great."

She pushed away, smiling. "Relax," she said. "You already got me. Remember?"

He grinned. "That was yesterday. I'm working on tonight now. Actually, I think you're going to be a long-term project."

In the living room he poured himself a drink while Beth put the rosebud in water.

"A long-term project," Warren said again, "in more ways than one. Kind of a handy arrangement. Occupation and preoccupation in one neat package."

She laughed. She liked laughing with Warren, loving him. But as for the long-term part, she wasn't sure. Perhaps she didn't have to be quite as sure anymore. But in one respect her relationship with Warren was undoubtedly going to last for a long time. As a legal problem, she was going to have real staying power.

The insurance problem was nearly settled now, because of Matthew. Because Matthew had lived long enough to confess, to implicate himself and Miles and

Eva in Jonathan's death, the outcome of the reopened investigation had not really been in doubt. But Paul's inheritance was an entirely different matter. The estate, all the Corey family property, was enmeshed in legal complications that would take years to unravel. Calvin's will had been meant to insure that the estate would be kept intact, family-owned and managed. But there was no one left now except Margaret and Carl—and Paul. Garfield and Pratt had wanted to know if Beth would take over the management as Paul's executrix, but her refusal had been immediate, unequivocal, and final. So now Garfield and Pratt had assumed the administration. But Warren was quite sure that someday everything could be sold, and part of the profit would be Paul's. But that day was many legal tangles away.

"Where's Paul?" Warren asked.

"In the sandbox with Gary. Building something. He's been fine all day, but last night he had nightmares again."

"Why don't you call him in? I'd like to have a chance to see him before we go. Mrs. Andersen coming tonight?"

"No. We're to drop him off there. She's sewing tonight, and Paul's more portable than her machine."

Beth went to the window in time to see what seemed to be the end of an altercation. Paul and the blond boy were standing nose to nose glaring at each other. She called, and watched long enough to see Paul leave the box and stomp towards the entry.

"Pratt called again today," Warren said. "The inventory's finished and next week everything goes into storage. Then they'll let the guards go, and Oma. She stayed for the inventory, but she's been anxious to get away. She has some relatives, it seems, in Oregon."

Beth shook her head wonderingly—over Oma's having courage enough to stay on at the Farmhouse with only the hired guards, over an Oma who seemed, in the empty Farmhouse, to have become a person, a person with plans and wishes of her own.

"Did you ask about Carl?" she asked. Carl had been restless, troublesome, at the private institution to which he had been sent, and had recently been changed to a licensed home for the retarded in the country.

"Yes, I did. He seems to be doing much better. He can be outdoors most of the time, and there are farm chores he can help with. It looks like a good solution. And Margaret is apparently much the same. Except that the lucid periods are much shorter. She's gone back farther now, to her childhood. She thinks that the doctor is her father. Seems to have forgotten all about Calvin and his infernal bargains."

Beth nodded and tried to smile but with limited success. Warren saw and came to her quickly, frowning. "I'm sorry. I didn't think—"

"It's all right. Really." She smiled brightly. "Here's Paul."

He stomped into the room, flushed and sandy. "Gary kicked down my Farmhouse," he announced.

"Your Farmhouse?" Beth tried to keep from frowning her anxiety.

"And what did you do?" Warren asked.

Paul grinned. "I sat on his spaceship." He dusted his hands together in satisfaction, examined them and put them behind his back. "Let's go to Mrs. Andersen's," he said. "You don't have to wash me first. Sand isn't dirt."

Beth took his hand and was starting towards the bathroom when Warren asked, "What was in your Farmhouse, Paul?"

"Just sand," Paul said. "Tomorrow I'm going to build a spaceship."

Warren looked at Beth and raised his eyebrows and his glass. "To tomorrow?" he said.

She smiled uncertainly, and then laughed. "To tomorrow," she said.